Strange Perfume

by

Wilson Loria

Published By

Breaking Rules Publishing

Softcover - 10051
Published by Breaking Rules Publishing
www.breakingruleswritingcompetitions.com
St Petersburg, Florida

~ *Acknowledgment* ~

First off, I believe I am grateful to the Universe. Why do I say that? It led and let me meet Nelson, the protagonist of *Strange Perfume*. Although this is a work of fiction, yes, Nelson was one of the most beautiful, living human beings I had ever met in my life. Nelson was more than a friend. He was definitely my mentor. He was the one who introduced me to so many unknown things. I was then a young man living in NYC. Nelson was the one who introduced me to old Hollywood films, the Opera, all sorts of ethnic food and Cuba, of course. Once, on a Saturday evening, he'd gone to one those now-defunct video stores, and rented Billy Wilder's *The Apartment* with Shirley MacLaine and Jack Lemmon. I was so tired that I fell asleep from beginning to end. No wonder, I had worked all morning and taken a *Capoeira* class (with Carlos, yes, he is in the story, too) that same day. To this date, I haven't seen it. I guess I can now easily stream it on my TV. Oh, boy, how life has undoubtedly changed so much since then. But my love and appreciation has not changed a bit for my dearest and unforgettable friend Nelson in spite of all these years.

I would like to express my gratitude for these three friends who have supported not only my both literary and theater careers, but also my life: David Boston, Carlos Guerriero, and Ciara Carinci. These human beings have always been there for me and I expect them to be for at least a century more.

I also thank Christopher Clawson-Rule from Breaking Rules Publishing, who believed in my story and has been doing tremendous work in the publishing business. Keep up the good work, Christopher.

Lastly, I thank my parents, Lourdes and Waldemar. Two human beings who are now part of the Universe, but who certainly understood, throughout their lives, what that *Strange Perfume* meant and still means to all of us.

To all the 'Nelsons' in the world

We're all of us sentenced to solitary confinement
inside our own skins -
Tennessee Williams

Something a little strange, that's what you notice
that she's not a woman like all the others
- Manuel Puig

Magically located on the main routes into and out of the Gulf of Mexico, Cuba was the last Spanish colony in the New World. Columbus landed in Cuba on its first voyage in 1492 and, probably enchanted by such beautiful earthly paradise, he might have wanted to stay and from there hop from island to island in the Caribbean. Oh, the tropics. He might have strolled its palm-shaded and whipped cream beaches, swum in that enchanting sapphire sea. He might have wished to ride a bamboo raft down its rivers or visited its waterfalls and bubbling brooks. Had he ever stopped to smell the air in Cuba? If he didn't, he was certainly an old fool.

Chapter 1

I was almost sixteen when I decided, without any apparent reason, to eat jarred baby food that was starting to invade the island. At home, there was an enormous pantry where *Papi* kept the *chorizos* -- of all kinds and sizes -- bacon, *jamón*, *frijoles*, *papas*, *tortillas*, coffee and condiments on a shelf on the right side. The baby food jars -- they were all for me to eat which I had made *Papi* buy one by one -- were kept on the left.

And at the table, dinner or lunchtime, I wouldn't stop talking about my favorite movie, *The Red Shoes*.

"Red, what, *niño*?" asked *Papi*.

"Her shoes. Her shoes were red. And they never stopped dancing."

"*Vamos*, eat."

"And the actress, Moira Shearer, playing Victoria Page is so beautiful. Her face, so fair... And her red hair... And her bare shoulders when she runs downstairs, flying off that balcony and falling right onto the railroad tracks..."

"*Niño*, stop talking and try to eat."

"And I myself could smack that shoemaker for selling her those shoes. That part was in Hans Christian Andersen's tale and they kept it in the film version..."

'It's getting cold."

"She is totally marveled by those shoes..."

"That food has to be eaten while it's still hot."

"At the end of the evening, the girl gets so tired but the red shoes are never tired. And they dance her out into alleys and around cities, over mountains and through fields, night and day. Bewitched and totally exhausted, the girl dies..."

"*Niño*. I think you are the one who's bewitched at this table. *Madre de Dios*."

"But the movie changes the fairy tale a little bit. The mean shoemaker becomes her ballet impresario..."

"*Hijo!*"

"And sometimes when I am at the movie house, I close my eyes and imagine María Félix playing Shearer's role as the prima ballerina..."

I loved María Félix in all those Mexican pictures. And those eyebrows of hers, under the biggest *sombreros* you could ever imagine. And how could I forget those eyebrows? I had even cut her face out of a movie magazine and glued it inside my locker at school, but some of my classmates found out about it and started to make fun of me. Most of them had big Cuban mulatto women's asses pinned upon their locker doors. To be honest, I did not care about Cuban mulatto women's asses at all.

By that time, of course, I liked women, but covered up with the most beautiful satin dresses, pearls -- don't even dare think of rhinestones -- around their ivory-colored necks and lots and lots of makeup on their delicate, pale, milky-white complexioned faces. I loved to steal my sister Gilda's lipstick and paint some of it on María Félix's lips on the picture. When I discovered that my aunt Mamita, who lived with us, also had a little bottle of mascara, I applied some to those famous María Félix's skinny, arched eyebrows. I accidentally spilled a few drops of it on María's forehead, resulting in a fake birthmark. Her eyebrows and forehead started to glitter from then on.

But, one day, my schoolmates discovered her in my locker. Scared to death, her expression changed immediately after they had opened the locker door, looking at her with their teasing eyes. I am sure she felt as though she was naked in front of their rude jokes and remarks. I was then to be known as the sissy of the class and became Nelsídia among those boys who thought they represented the most macho breed of Cuba. Please... And I then had to win back my respect from them. That's when I started giving my best in the games, showing that I was also able to take any violent blow to my body. That's when I felt it getting stronger and stronger: I had a fight with one of them and fortunately broke half of one of his front teeth. As a reward, my respectability was regained. Yeah, that simple...

***

"It's a pity María Félix could never dance. Maybe Alicia Alonso would have been able to play the role... *Papi?*"

"*Sí?*"

"I can't stand those people at school talking

about Russian politics."

"I know. That'll end soon. It's just a fad."

"I think the only Russian name that my mind can tolerate to bear is the impresario's in the movie, Boris Lermontov."

"Stop talking nonsense and eat."

***

At the Military Academy, I studied public relations, history -- my favorite subject -- languages and economics. But I simply loved the physical education classes. Well, what I really liked were those twenty minutes we had to shower and get dressed for the first classes in the morning. Looking at all those bodies, I looked down and examined mine. I was jealous of them. I had been a very sick baby, stricken with meningitis at a very early age, and not even the family's doctor expected me to survive. But I had managed to defy Medicine and the proof of it was that I now was in the locker room, comparing my own body to the bodies of my classmates. At times, I would pretend I was getting dressed, but what I really did was observe those young, tight-muscled bodies.

I never forgot this tall, mulatto kid, about sixteen, who every time he took a shower, would dry himself with the thickest towel I had ever seen in my life. Then, he would rub some Vaseline on his penis. I remember him massaging his member with the scented oil, and looking around as to make sure someone was watching him. I was, behind my locker door. I guess I was spying on him. Something stirred inside me when I watched that little show of exhibitionism. Inexplicably, I liked it. I wanted it.

***

"And Lermontov asks Victoria why she wants to dance, and she smartly answers him, 'Why do you want to live?'"

"What's got into you tonight, Nelson?"

"And Victoria Page falls in love with the young conductor Julian Crester. They then decide to elope and get married. Boris is extremely jealous of them. And towards the end of the film, she comes back to the stage..."

"I'm bringing your plate back to the kitchen."

"And now she has to choose between the love for her husband and love for the ballet."

"Enough!"

And that was exactly what the manager of that fleabag movie house in my *barrio*, the Cine Strand, had also shouted at me when I walked in to see *The Red Shoes* for the three hundredth time. He was sick of my face, I guess.

***

"I'm not going to repeat it again. *Coma!*"

"Beets? I hate those."

"What is it that you want to eat, then?"

"Apricot with apple."

"But you haven't eaten solid food for months! And I worked so hard in the kitchen to prepare this food for you and your brothers and, in the end; you crave only those things that do not kill anybody's hunger."

"If they didn't kill it, all babies in the whole world would be dead by now, *Papi*."

And convinced by my brilliant observation, *Papi* would get up from the table, walk through the corridor, which linked the dining room and the pantry, and searched out the apricot and apple baby food jar. The poor man always forgot to turn on the naked light bulb hanging in there and tried to read all those labels in the dark. Sometimes, he would realize he had gotten the wrong jar just when he was already by the sink in the kitchen, looking for a bottle opener.

Then, he would open two of those and pour the contents on my favorite little porcelain plate with an engraving of a lady sitting by the shade of a fig tree and two huge gray dogs running after each other. Still mushing it with a fork, he proudly brought me the paste on the plate as if he himself had just prepared it with fresh fruit picked from our backyard, where we had mango, guava and avocado trees.

Both *Papi* and Grandma -- when she still had enough energy -- would prune them, singing Augustin Lara's *María Bonita,* a song written for Mexican actress María Félix. We also had a kitchen garden where Mother grew her own carrots, cabbages and big, succulent plum tomatoes. Grandma loved picking the guavas because she said that by picking them herself, the preserves she eventually made with them would turn out tastier.

Grandma made coconut sweets, candy, fruitcakes and preserves -- her specialty -- while sipping her sacrosanct, daily glass of red wine before her afternoon nap. I loved it when Grandma let the overripe guavas boil in a big steel pan, which simmered on our stove for endless hours. They would dissolve like jelly, and you could even see the white and yellow tiny seeds letting go of the pulp of the fruit. Every single room in the house would be magically infused with the guava smell, which naturally would assault our noses. I also liked to come near Grandma and kiss her on the cheek, so I could smell the guava that had deliciously perfumed her clothes. Her hair gave off a delicious smell of clove. Grandma would fill tens of jars with the homemade paste that we would consume little by little for months on end.

My mania for baby food turned out to be known as one of the brattiest things that I had ever invented since I was a child. Yes, I was a spoiled brat.

***

"And what you see in the last scene is Victoria asking Julian to take her shoes off her feet, which by now are smeared by blood. In Andersen's tale, the frail little girl, tired of dancing without a rest, asks an angel to saw off both her feet. And so he does."

***

Once Mother pinched my neck in front of everybody -- which hurt me inside the most -- just because I did not stop talking about the film while we were having dinner. And between spoonfuls of the flan she had prepared for dessert, what had irritated Mother -- months later she confessed to me during a little chat over coffee in the afternoon -- was that I imitated every actor's voice in the film and she loathed the fact that I had also imitated the leading actress's voice at the table. The voice of a charming, frail and young girl.

Chapter 2

I had a part-time job in the afternoon at the Department of Buildings and Bridges in the City Hall after classes at the Military Academy. Sometimes, I would not go to work and sneak into the movie house. I then made up an excuse at home and in the office. I was damn good at making up stories. They all believed me all right.

I wanted badly to leave Cuba. I just couldn't believe in all those promises or the biggest lie that Cuba would be the first Latin American industrial country, the Land Reform, the Party, the Youth Group. My heart just couldn't bear that those ugly pale men, with their odd language, getting drunk on and addicted to our *aguardiente* were invading the island. I would cry just by looking at all those beautiful houses that were starting to be inhabited by three, four, even five families. A few houses didn't even have running water, forcing them to pump buckets for cooking, showering or flushing the only hole on the ground that now served them as toilet.

But before leaving for the United States, I needed to do something. In my bedroom, I spent Saturday mornings listening to *Papi's* old records of operas trying to get an idea, a clue of what to do in order to take vengeance on what was happening to my beloved Cuba. I would forget the record playing and then the needle would keep scratching and Mother, irritated, would ask from outside if I was asleep. I would answer no and play the records once again. And as if I had heard a click in my mind and along with Rodolfo in La Bohème, I threw out my chest, "*Fuoco!*"

And stolen from *Papi's* stove, I carried a little match in the inside pocket of my jacket, along with an empty matchbox, on a Saturday afternoon, the day nobody was around, to the Department of Buildings. I had the keys to my office. It was kind of creepy and damp in there and I could hear only my footsteps on the waxed floor along those long corridors. Unwillingly, while unlocking the office door, I dropped the key and the match. I didn't want to turn on the lights; although, I was sure that there was nobody around. For a few seconds, I searched for the match. I had brought only one with me. Silly me! When the key hit the floor, it made a metallic sound that echoed everywhere in the building. And after scattering a few sheets of paper here and there, before my eyes, I first set fire to a sheet and immediately burned to ashes the entire map of the city's sewage system, the drawings of those statues of Russian heroes to be erected soon, the plans of the Guantánamo's Naval Base, the model of the Foreign Affairs Ministry, the plan of the Cemetery of Colón, of the famous Tropicana cabaret that would be closed with its employees sent to work in the mango and sugar cane plantations, the plan of the Fiber Manufacturers and of La Polar's Brewery. Today, I think I could have set fire to the whole of Havana. And I am sure I would have played two enormous *maracas* had I had enough time. I would have played them to celebrate the fall of the city, which I would watch from the balcony of the building. And, who knows, that could have been the end of the Revolution itself. I could have been a hero.

I closed the door behind me and ran as fast as I could without looking back. Reaching the end of Prado Promenade, I crossed Monte Street and passed Fraternidad Park with that enormous spreading tree. Almost out of breath, I raised my eyes and the only thing I saw was the marble Indian Maiden Fountain with her Greek face and a feathered headdress. Out of the corner of my eye, I saw the José Martí Theatre on Dragones Street. By now, I thought I was going to die. My heart raced not only from so much running, but also from fear of being caught after setting fire to those documents in my office. If they found out about me, I would never be able to leave Cuba. And they never did.

I was happy when I finally reached the most beautiful building on the Prado, the Capitol. I greeted both statues representing Labor and Virtue at its main entrance. The Prado had never seemed to me so infinitely long. Stopping for a few seconds on the sidewalk, I noticed a small ring of people listening to a man playing the accordion in front of the famous García Lorca Theatre, where I always hurried to catch performances of the National Ballet and the Opera. Now I was almost at Central Park with its exquisite marble fountains, benches and that majestic statue of José Martí. I looked up and told the statue what I had just done. I swear I saw him nodding his head yes as if he agreed with me.

With José Martí's approval on my mind, I continued running, passing bronze lions, office buildings, restaurants and shops. At the foot of the Prado, I could smell hints of the sea. I rushed into our house and flew straight to my room, locking the door behind me.

On the following day, after my last breakfast with my family, we all left for the port where I was to set sail for the United States. It was still quite easy to leave Cuba without any major problems, for it was only the beginning o the Communist revolution. It was its second anniversary.

***

"*Papi?*"

"Yes, *hijo*," he answered, keeping his eyes on the slice of a ripe papaya as he meticulously scraped off its tiny black seeds.

"I only wanted to thank you."

"For what?"

"For buying me the ticket."

"*De nada, hijo.* I knew that sooner or later I'd have to do that."

"Please, don't cry, *Papi.*"

"I'm not."

And wiping his cheeks with the back of his right hand, he got up from his chair, and went to the stove to turn it off, since a pot of milk was about to boil over. Then, he poured himself some more coffee and came back to the table. We were left alone in the kitchen. Grandma, Mami, Gilda, and Mamita had rushed into their bedrooms to finish dressing.

"When did you buy it, *Papi*?"

"I went to the port two weeks ago."

"Why?"

"First, because you've already mentioned that you could not go on living here and I myself can see why not. And secondly, deep inside, I know that this is the best I can do for you right now. Send you to the United States."

"What if I won't be able to come back... ever..."

He did not answer me. He just turned his face, hiding his welled-up eyes, adding, "We'd better get going, *hijo*."

Our trip to the port was quiet and fast. We all fit in Mamita's boyfriend Blanco's car and we kept silent as if we all had lost our ability to talk. Only now and then, Gilda would produce a sniffing sound with her nose. Hugging and kissing all of them was painful. I boarded the ship without looking back. On deck, I smelled something I could not identify at first, but I knew for sure that I had already smelled it in the company of my family. That aroma was to follow me all my life.

Gripping with both hands at the iron railing on the ship, a big caramel-colored steamer called *Corcovado*, I saw my sister Gilda -- who never did leave Cuba -- wiping her delicate eyes with an embroidered linen kerchief, Grandma, aunt Mamita, Mami and *Papi*. My brothers Juan and Johnny couldn't come with us; they had been working in the countryside for some time then. Johnny's wife, Dora, and their child and my godson Enriquito had to stay home, since he had been running a high fever. My oldest brother Oswaldo was already in the United States and so was my sister Carmela, who, years before, had married an American man. They had a little boy, Brad, whom we all called *el americanito*.

When I saw them all weeping and sniffing their noses in unison, my hands clutched the railing in pain. I could see my little family standing among the swaying crowd at the wharf. And as if it were a sign for me to cheer up, a sailor was passing by at that moment with his transistor on, glued to his ear. I couldn't help listening to a snatch of the song: Mimi in La Bohème. I immediately raised my eyes and as if looking for something behind the clouds, I asked whatever was up there to also help me live.

To my surprise, at the port, my family took out from a big wicker basket little objects that sparkled against the morning sun. I swear I thought they were bringing me little Coca-Cola bottles filled up with rum, so I could drink during the trip, but when I rubbed my eyes hard, I could finally focus on what they all had in their hands: short, fat jars. They didn't have a chance to give me what they had brought me as farewell gifts: each of them held in their hands baby food jars with different flavors and preserves that Grandma had made especially for me the night before.

Chapter 3

La Habana

4 January 1961

Mi querido hijo:

The end of the year and the first days of the new year, which has just been born, find us in good health, in spite of the uncertainty our country is currently going through. Mankind and the Cuban people especially deserve rest after such a truceless battle. Our people wish to live in peace and all this week, they celebrated Fidel and his guerrillas entering La Habana in the first days of 1959. That was when he took hold of the city, changing radically everybody's life on the island. Forever.

We don't know how we are going to get news from you, since our country has broken off diplomatic relations with the. U.S.. Maybe God will send us a messenger to put us in contact, be it through a letter from you, Carmela or Oswaldo who are my dearest children roaming those foreign lands.

As for looking for a job, it would be better if you could find something through your brother Oswaldo. He may have many connections, since he's been in that country for a while now. But I hope that living with our friend Odilia, in New York, will work out perfectly well. If not, you can take a bus and go straight to your sister Carmela in Miami, which would make us be more at peace. I hope Odilia may be like a mother to you.

And here's a note from your real Mother:

Dear hijo:

Yesterday, I went to pay one more installment for your record player. I paid 8,50 pesos, so now we still owe 40.

Hijo, browsing through your record jackets, I see that La Bohème, Carmen and La Forza Del Destino are missing. I found out, through a few friends of yours, that you sold Carmen and La Forza for 25 pesos and now I wonder if you also sold La Bohème. Mamita told me that a good friend of yours by the name Pepe has it, but this muchacho hasn't called or returned the record yet.

Love,

La Doña

P.S. -- After writing you these lines, I found Pepe's telephone number and gave him a call. He told me, yes, he has La Forza Del Destino and one of these days, he'll bring it back. And he also bought Carmen from you a few months before you left Cuba. I told him that I'd like to have all of your things together, in case you come back home, hijo. Pepe told me you've written him a few lines and you know how much he likes Tebaldi, too. He said that you wrote him about the opera you went to see the other day at the Metropolitan House.

Besos

Wishing you prosperity and luck during this year and know that you can count on your father's cariño, always.

Papi.

Chapter 4

"Walter, I have to confess to you something: my parents do not know that I am here with you in New York. I am so glad we met when you were on vacation in Cuba. I knew we would be good friends the moment we met at *El Carmelo*. I certainly don't know how to thank you for letting me stay here until I get my own place."

"..."

"Yes, I mean it. Thank you so much. They wanted me to live either with my oldest brother Oswaldo, in Maine, or my sister Carmela, who is now in Miami. I never wanted to do that. I thought, once I was out of my parents', I wanted to be on my won. I've always dreamed of it, always wanted to try that. If a frail young girl could live on her own, in La Bohème, why can't I? My parents think I am staying with this lady, Odilia, who's been their friend for the longest time."

"..."

"Sure, I have, Walter. It's my one and only favorite opera. And when the frail girl is dying, no matter how many times I've heard it, I always get goose bumps. I know it sounds morbid, but that's the act I like the most. I heard it thousands of times when my father played his old opera records while preparing his famous meals. His Sunday lunches give off aromas that waft from the kitchen and mingle with the perfume of the tropical fruit trees in our backyard. If you happen to be under them where we have a hammock tied up around two thick mango trees when *Papi* is cooking and smell the aroma of his condiments frying and sizzling on the stove that is a real treat in itself. Seasoning is *Papi's* forte. When he is nor reading or writing for his magazine -- he owns a small magazine in Havana, no more than 30 pages an issue -- he is always busy slicing onions, washing chili peppers under the kitchen faucet and carving off the seeds of ripe red, yellow and green *pimientos*, picked in my mother's kitchen garden."

"..."

"I know. I know. It sounds crazy but I love my records of La Bohème so much that I had to bring them with me. The box they are in is so special. On the lid is a lovely picture of Mimi wearing a red felt bonnet and nice earrings, and Rodolfo is standing, looking bewitched, beside her. The earrings are laminated with chips of real mother-of-pearl. They are in that trunk. Found them?

"…"

"You're serious? The Metropolitan Opera House? Tonight? Of course, I want to go. You didn't need to ask. But, first, I have to take a nap, though. It's freezing out there. I need a couple of hours under the blankets. Is that all right with you?"

"…"

"Oh, look at that, Walter. This is the first time I see snow. It looks so beautiful from here. Oh, Manhattan… Look at those roofs covered with snow. I've only heard of it all my life through my father's opera records and seen in films. I feel like going out this minute and eating it."

"…"

"Yes, I'm sorry. I am yawning at you. The cruise was long and tiring and the ship's cabin was not comfortable at all. I got seasick a couple of times during the trip. In fact, it looked much more like a battleship (or a huge raft?) and felt like the cruise would never end. Walter, did you know that cruise ships carry coffins in their hulls?"

"..."

"No, *querido. Gracias.* I am not hungry. Maybe a glass of warm milk? That'd be nice. We can eat something light before the theater, can't we? Ok. Let me take a nap."

"..."

"Oh, yes. I really needed it. I'm ready. Are we walking? Down Central Park to the Metropolitan? Can we take a picture of me wearing this coat, scarf and hat so that I send a copy to Cuba?"

"..."

"Great. Look, Walter! José Martí's statue right here just like on Prado Promenade. *Papi* won't believe me when I write him about it. Oh, my. Oh, my. The Metropolitan Opera House! Walter. Look. Touch my heart. I am going to faint. Of course I don't mind standing in line. I don't mind if it is going to take one hour, one day, one month, or one year. I am standing in line for La Bohème. "

"...."

"Look, Water. This guy behind us. Not bad, huh?" He is talking to me, Walter."

"..."

"Este maricón quiere que guardemos su lugar en la fila para él."

" ... "

"Walter! He can speak Spanish!"

("Well if that is such an inconvenience for you and your friend to hold a place in line for me, I shall ask someone else. I am awfully sorry!")

"Walter! I don't know where to hide my face. He can speak Spanish! What should I say, Walter?"

" ... "

"Yes, my friend and I will see that nobody takes your place. I'm Nelson. This is my friend Walter."

("I'm Ronald. How do you do? What beautiful hands you have. Small, smooth and a bit cold. Want to come to my apartment, which is only two blocks down here, so we can warm your hands a bit?")

"Walter. What should I do? He is proposing to me right here, in front of you. Huh? The New York way. Oh, my. What should I do, Walter? You stay here, watching our places in line? Ok, Ronald, let's go..."

And we did go to his apartment where I was almost eaten alive, not by Ronald, but by his two huge German shepherds guarding the door. The apartment was small for a person with two dogs. Except for some work on his peeling bathroom ceiling, it was a cozy apartment. It is almost one hundred years old, he told me.

Soon we were back to the Opera House. We stepped into the hall and I asked Walter to pinch my arm so I could make sure I was not in Cuba, dreaming of all that. No, it was happening to me. It was true.

Throughout the opera, Ronald kept holding my hand and whispered in my ear that I had the coldest little hands he had never before held. Placing my hand on his own crotch I, out of the blue, cried out along with Rodolfo, "*Fuoco!*" I was glad that the drums and the strings were playing a very loud passage which luckily had the power of outdoing my own shaky voice. Walter was so immersed in the opera that either he didn't see a thing or he was playing dumb. I never knew for sure. Soon, Ronald's penis started throbbing through my fingers, hand and arm towards my heart, which in turn, was already racing wildly like a track horse. At the intermission, Ronald and I went to the men's room where he grabbed me by the waist, pushed me inside one of those toilet stalls, and kissed me while proposing to me if I wanted to come and live with him. He was quickly and desperately in love with me. I could not believe my ears, right on the first day in New York, *Mary Dugan*, I had already caused someone to fall for me that way.

Yes, I accepted his invitation and we lived like a married couple for almost five years, spending the nights talking about life, playing opera to our friends, visiting his family in Baltimore and once in a while we would call Cuba and chat with my family.

One day, I decided to take a few days off my job. At that time, I was already working in the real estate business and my work schedule was fairly flexible. I then planned to spend my vacation in Puerto Rico. Ronald could not come with me because he was about to be promoted to accountant manager at this big firm downtown Manhattan.

When I came back from Puerto Rico, it was clear that there was no way that Ronald and I could continue living together. And we split in a very amicable way: no dishes were smashed on the kitchen floor and he kept his two dogs. Deep down, both of us knew that we absolutely had to separate.

Chapter 5

La Habana

6 March

Mi querido hijito:

You don't know how happy I am to write these lines to you. I miss you so much. It was a day like today, a very unusual cold afternoon when I saw you boarding that ship and we waited till it disappeared at sea, blowing a long mournful whistle.

Tranquility reigns in our old big house. It's not that your Mother, La Doña, and I are much more in love with each other now. No. It's that we are simply too old to be constantly at war and, as you know, all battles reach an end. There are no winners or losers around here, though, and you, better than anyone else, know how much I long for peace and when, once in a while she starts nagging, I just pretend to be deaf. No one will ever be able to reproach me for picking on your Mother.

Mamita.... I have just shown her your letter. She gets older and more *puta* every single day. She is still involved with Blanco without any hope of landing him. She is here, beside me and has just blown three kisses into the air and planted one right on my left ear which made me temporarily deaf. She told me those kisses are for you. Mamita is so in shape. Blanco is definitely a happy and lucky man. Yesterday, she came out of her room wearing this enormous low-cut dress, without a girdle, or panties. The dress was a see-through, but I still haven't fallen for her, if that was her main objective. I think she definitely doesn't have the class to be your stepmother. Gilda, your sister, told her that nobody around here needs one, since La Doña is still living and in good health; although, sometimes she pretends to be sick and makes up indescribable pains, testing the waters to get an idea of *"what kind of funeral services you all are going to have for me."* The other day, your mother, for no reason, smashed those china plates -- the ones I inherited from your Grandmother -- on the kitchen floor, *hijo.*

Your bothers Johnny and Juan have me greatly worried. My soul tells me something bad is going on with those young men. They keep quiet. The other day, on the phone, they wouldn't tell me what they've been doing for the government as if they were keeping war secrets. They are involved with the public construction battalion, that I know. A week later, they sent us a bottle of wine. Bulgarian wine. Can you believe that?

Gilda, your sister, is mad at you because she was the only one you forgot to mention in your letter. You should write to her, *hijo*.

A very tight hug and thousands of kisses from your old man.

P.S. -- *Your mother has just yelled from the kitchen that she will write you tomorrow.*

Chapter 6

When I arrived at the hotel in Puerto Rico on a Monday, I immediately unpacked and went out for a walk. Two guys outside this movie house wanted a threesome and why not? Nice French and Puerto Rican guys. I had a lot of trouble having an erection, but grass helped get rid of hang-ups. On my first day in Puerto Rico, I ended up going to bed exhausted at four in the morning.

On Tuesday, off I went to the beach and started making friends. It was incredible how sociable I was when I was alone. Bumping heads by accident with somebody in the water, we at once made out and romance started right at the beach. Many queens around were clearly jealous. His name was Joaquín, or Jackie. Soon we were in my hotel room, making love all over the room. He was a wild kid.

On Wednesday, I went back to the beach at one in the afternoon. Handing me a *piña colada*, Jackie turned out to be a little too possessive. However, he invited me to see a show at the Cabaret with Iris Chacón that night. It was very funny. I had a little scene with a stubborn Puerto Rican queen who would not take no for an answer. And popper's galore. Suddenly somebody came in and I went crazy. What a pair of eyes. Funny enough, he turned out to be Dino, Jackie's brother. And I froze.

On Thursday, I went to the beach again in the afternoon, walking the streets like a zombie. Dino was there with Jackie's friends. I was immediately nervous, but played it cool. In the morning, I had promised myself to have fun and no sex. We all swam in the nude and lots of water playing. Dino did not come to the water with us, though. I was drying myself on the beach when I saw Dino getting closer and closer to me. Things got very hot when, out of the blue, he whispered in my ear, "I was supposed to leave for New York today, but decided not to and came to the beach to really meet you. My brother told me about you, Nelson." I was even more nervous. All the queens were all eyes. Telling his brother Jackie that he was getting married real soon, Dino kept looking me in the eye. I froze once again and stayed at the beach, floating on a cloud, and deep inside hoping that he would miss his plane.

I went back to my hotel for a nap. I needed it. I passed out, really. We all went to dinner at the *Metropolis*, which served very good Cuban food. And off to the *Abbey* at midnight. The place was packed and more grass and poppers on the dance floor. As I walked back to my hotel alone, I started thinking of both Ronald and our love affair. What was I doing? Was it fair to Ronald? He was probably waiting for me, looking through the window, witnessing the coming spring with the snow thawing and flowers blooming. Was that a tacky thought or what? And looking up the sky, I saw the most beautiful starry night. The cobblestone streets were a bit slippery because of an unexpected tropical rain that had fallen in the early evening. I was feeling dizzy not only because of the drinks and the grass, which undoubtedly had something in it, but also my unfaithfulness. And the only thing I could do then was to scream out loud as if I could be heard in New York, "I'm sorry, Ronald! *Perdóname!* Forgive me!" Dogs started barking. And a few lights at the houses nearby were turned on as I breathlessly ran to my hotel. While running, I could smell the salt coming from the beach no more than two blocks from there. I staggered up to my room by four in the morning, drunk, confused and sad.

Phone rang at 8 o'clock on Friday morning. Wrong room. I could have killed them. They called again from downstairs five minutes later to tell me that I had to change rooms before noon. I packed and moved to the new room, which was gorgeous, wild and red. Too much. It was pouring outside. At about one in the afternoon, I was trying to take a nap when the phone rang again. I could have killed them again. And calling from downstairs, the voice on the other side of the line sounded familiar. Dino! I literally flew downstairs.

When we were walking upstairs to my room, my heart started beating faster. As a matter of fact, I felt my blood pumping through me. While trying to open the door, only then had I realized that the key was left inside the room. I rushed back downstairs and asked the bellboy to please open the door. When he finally unlocked it, I myself opened it slowly. It was dark inside because the heavy red curtains were drawn shut, and the room smelled of something I quite could not recognize at once. A strange perfume.

I invited Dino to come in. However, we had to wait a little while at the door so we could get used to the darkness of the room. Soon both of us started to look for the switch. I almost tripped over a *chaise* near the bed while he was touching the wall; although, not as gently as he touched me afterwards. During our private Switch Hunt, he did not say a word, making me a little apprehensive and for a moment, I thought I was in the room all by myself. I think he was smiling. I could not see his face in the dark.

It took us a while to find the switch that was on the right side of the door. I had moved to that room in the morning and I did not know exactly where the switch was. Dino reached for it and the room lit up at once. I thought maybe the light bulb on the ceiling gave off that scent. I still could not define.

How beautiful Dino was. His skin was very tanned, but extremely white on his bikini line. I could not imagine his fair skin fading back to his natural color after a few days. His green eyes matched his shirt, his malicious eyes. A well-built nose, the kind of nose you would feel like biting right away. His neck smelled as fresh as a baby's. His teeth, ivory. His mouth, delicious. It tasted like honey for days.

Dino had decided not to go to New York and missed his plane. And as he told his brother at the beach, he had come to marry me. And a frightening thought once again crossed my mind: "Ronald! What am I going to tell him?" On the one hand, I certainly needed to think it all over, but the most probable answer to that situation I saw myself in was: the same way my love affair with Ronald had started, it was now coming to an end... quickly. Our love affair had worn off as so many others we both knew. It wouldn't be easy for the two of us to get separated, of course, but I trusted Ronald to be an understanding, mature and kind man. I also knew that he would agree with me that our separation was certainly unavoidable. One thing was completely sure: I was desperately in love with Dino.

Dino jumped into bed and as if he were about to take a dive, tossed around and kept lying on his back, looking at the ceiling. I saw him examining the light bulb on the ceiling, and I thought he had noticed also that the bulb was different.

I sat down in the *chaise* near the bed, looking at him. I still couldn't believe he had come back to me. Then, he reached for the pack of cigarettes, on my nightstand. He lit one, inhaled the smoke, savoring it. I kept staring at Dino. I guess I was literally studying him from head to toe. I scrutinized every single pore of his. I stood up and turned on the radio. I could not believe my ears: Mimi was singing her head off.

He looked at the smoke circles he puffed into the air. Suddenly, he rested the cigarette on the crystal ashtray. And stretching his left arm, his hand came close to me. I felt that he was calling me without saying a word. He grabbed my hand and made a comment, "It is such a small, smooth and cold hand." No wonder, I was shaking inside. He was just making the gesture of what he wanted the most at that moment: he wanted me... and so he would for the next thirteen years.

Chapter 7

La Habana

5 June

Querido Nelson:

I am going crazy in the house, walking in circles: from the front door to the kitchen and from the kitchen to the front door. At times, I think I have water in my brain for thinking so much of the situation I am facing now.

There is no other way but retire, since they stopped publishing the *Información* magazine, and the National Press is not taking on old journalists and management's order is to get all of us to retire. I will certainly not be an exception, *hijo*. And I don't know when *Comércio y Economía* magazine will be out this month, or if it will ever hit the newsstands. I have only collected fifty pesos so far for advertising and my only salvation raft was the peasants, whose funds have just been frozen in the banks, which, in turn, are doomed to disappear as an organized institution. To date, I haven't run out of cash because I keep billing the National Press and, Thank God, I have a little money saved.

I can see that you put on ten pounds at least, and it's funny to see you wearing those thick winter clothes. Your eyes are a bit more piercing, you're taller, more elegant and above all, you look more mature. What's that cigarette doing, tucked between your fingers? On the picture, it is funny to see the smoke circles -- that you may have just puffed -- in the air above you. I also see that you are growing a fine mustache, which makes me think of Mr. Lermontov's own mustache. *Gracias* for the picture, *hijo*. Before I forget, I must tell you that I've become the best customer at Cine Strand. Do you miss it? I have something to tell you about that movie house. Whenever you enter it, there is -- in the air -- a smell of solvent damp sheets from a mimeograph machine. Probably from the flyers they make announcing the new feature film they show every week.

The relations between the U.S. and Cuba are going from bad to worse, I guess. But your Mother is not discouraged at all, though, getting ready to go to the U.S. in October. She may have the luck to kiss and hug you very soon. Her kisses and hugs will also be mine.

I am going to the kitchen now. There is this big steak waiting for me. It's only six-thirty in the evening, and my stomach is already growling.

Regards to your friends and Odilia.

Your *viejito*.

P.S. -- *Please write your Mother and give her some advice, hijo. She is driving me nuts. I feel like I'm trapped. I don't know what else I can do. Leave her? I think this trip to the U.S. will do our old La Doña some good.*

Chapter 8

Dino and I left Puerto Rico for New York, to all the *girls'* amazement. We wanted to spend our honeymoon in some place as exotic as San Juan. After making arrangements at work, where I convinced my boss -- I had always been good at making up stories -- that the real estate business in New Orleans was to be checked in person, Dino and I eloped to the Mardi Gras City.

And off we went. It was a wonderful trip. We took turns at the wheel of the red convertible Buick we had rented. Sometimes we would switch places with the car in motion, and I swear that I twice had the impression that Dino had little wings on his back. I was afraid of that particular game but, luckily, nothing terrible happened. The nights were unbelievably clear, and the stars followed us all the way every single night. They were certainly a pleasant company. Dino's kisses smelled magically of something I could not recognize. A familiar smell, though.

In Ocean Springs, we went to a motel, whose bed had a mosquito netting. Wrapping himself up in it as if he were a bat that had suddenly been granted with sight, he would get his face near mine and tried kissing or biting my face. Sticking his tongue through one of the holes on the net, he licked my cheeks, which by now were wet with salty tears. A little drunk on wine and stoned, he did that once in the nude. His penis, also caught in the net, looked like a trapped and confused little humming bird. I laughed so hard. Silly Dino. Outside the room, we drank rum-cocos and tried to balance ourselves in a big hammock. He then spoke about his dream of being a poet. And the heat oozed unbearably through the streets of town.

In New Orleans, we ended up going to a hotel that resembled a rooming house. It was an old Tudor-style home with walls of dusty, light red bricks. At the entrance, an old black man with white, shiny and over-brilliantined hair welcomed you. There was a small slanting skylight which, together with the two lamps on the desk, helped illuminate the reception area. The interior however was always dusky. Three shuttered French doors opened directly to the backyard, where an old white bathtub served as a pond for a couple of frogs living there. The frogs made fun of the residents by screaming and showing their tongues at every single window at night. Purposely, the backyard actually resembled a tamed little jungle with ferns, rubber and banana trees and cages all around. There were two blue macaws and one parrot, which turned out to be as noisy as Bourbon Street itself. The hotel was run by a woman who, from the moment Dino and I stepped into it, did not stop talking about her city and how sorry she was that we had arrived on Monday, leaving us just one day of festivities. With a cigarette tucked in her fingers and rollers on the thinnest hair I had ever seen on a woman, she effusively talked about New Orleans (Momus balls, her relatives dying of yellow fever, her family losing every cent they had, girls carrying black cat's bones in their purses, Marie Laveau, the voodoo priestess, and two-horse carriages all over town). Dino quickly grew impatient. He wanted to go straight up to our room for a quick shower.

She finally gave us the keys to our room. The old man helped us carry our bags. To go upstairs, we had to take this elevator. I was afraid of it. The iron-gate did not lock and you had to bang it shut.

Our room was on the third floor and when we first walked in, the room reeked of Pine Sol. A black armoire with cracked mirrors on its doors. A graceless black dresser matched the armoire. It had gilt knobs, which were painted on with some indescribable paint, probably the same one used on the walls. A swinging naked light bulb -- just like the one we had in our pantry in Cuba. There was also a ceiling fan, a massive white iron bed with a light purple headboard and tumbled pillows. Old, faded blue sheets covered the bed. Beside the queen-sized bed, a washstand with rosebuds painted on the pitcher and bowl in which there were empty bottles of gin. Dull green blinds. The walls were mustard-colored, but there was something else on them that I could not believe.

I asked the black porter what those "spots" on the walls were and he told me a fascinating story. Once, in that room, lived an old lady, who in her forties had dreamed of marrying a wealthy man, but had never been that lucky. Time passed, her beauty wilted and her pastime changed to going to the basement of the hotel and browsing through old magazines, which the residents would leave outside their doors. The old lady used to cut out the faces of Hollywood stars, unscrupulously dismembering their bodies with a long sharp pair of scissors. A few of them ended up losing their necks, though. One day, she confided in him that the reason she cut out all those faces of handsome actors and beautiful actresses and pasted them on the walls of her room was because she had faith that by staring at them night and day, the baby, she was now carrying in her belly, was probably going to be born handsome as well. The old crazy lady went away, leaving her Hollywood stars pasted up on the walls of that room. A few days later, it seemed that it was totally impossible to scrape them out and the only smart solution they could find was slapping a fresh coat of paint on them. However, if you looked harder, you could spot a few smiles here and there like ghostly and milky-white faces grinning at you. Near the bathroom door, yes, there she was... María Félix. One of her pictures had luckily also been glued among all those Hollywood stars.

On the following morning, Dino wanted to sleep late and decided to take a walk by myself. Bourbon Street was packed by nine-thirty in the morning, and everyone was already holding a drink. I walked past bar after bar. At one of the striptease joints was a woman at the door showing her tits to the passerby. In the morning? Couples were openly kissing and a lot of drunk people lying on the sidewalks. I walked to Jackson Square. It was happily crowded with street performers and palm readers under their big colorful beach umbrellas. I looked for one, then. Why not? When I got to the table of the palm reader I felt comfortable with, she was leaving, trying to get out from under her beautiful star-decorated umbrella without messing her hairdo. She had long dark brown hair and black mascara around her liquid green eyes. Approaching her, I said, "Please. Don't leave. You're such a beautiful woman. I want to speak to you."

She was visibly touched by my comment. Asking me to take a seat, she said her name was Shannon and asked me if I wanted to have my palm read or Tarot cards. I chose the cards.

"I don't tell past. Only your future. Are you sure you want to know about it?"

"Very much."

"Cut them in two. Now, look at this card... It says, "Do not pay attention to so many money details.'"

"What do you mean?"

"You are in the real estate business, aren't you? Don't worry about its ups and downs."

I couldn't believe my ears.

"You have a wonderful ability to work very hard without breaking your back. Go on with that, and money will come soon. Save some, though. You will need it for your future."

"My love life?"

"Look at that card. You see? That means you're the one who goes ahead with your relationships. Do you want me to continue?"

"Please."

"The person you're currently involved with will unfortunately have to face a horrendous health problem. However, the person does not know about it yet. It'll take some time."

"Is the person faithful to me?"

"You're the only one to answer that. Are you?"

"I'm learning to be."

"Look. You'll also have to watch your health. Not a big concern, though. Just stay away from the bottle."

I kept quiet.

"You're not from the U.S.."

"... from Cuba."

"Nelson, darling, you'll be receiving not so comforting news from your country in a very near future."

"*Mami? Papi?*"

"Easy, easy... Time heals everything, honey."

"Do you see anything good?"

"Oh, yes. Look at that one, further from you. Sex."

"What about it?"

"Lots of it," she said, winking at me. "Anything else you'd like to ask me?"

"I guess that'd be it. How much will it be?"

"You see. We are a union of palm readers at this square. We do not charge, but accept donations from 5 to 10 dollars."

I gave her a ten-dollar bill and left. At the hotel, I found Dino as mad as a hornet. He was on the brink of crying. I myself started to cry, thinking of Shannon's words about Dino.

Yes, we did walk down to Jackson Square, to the French Market, to Café du Monde and had a typical *café au lait*. Yes, we did take a ride on the famous steamboat Natchez. Yes, we did go to the queer balls on Tuesday night; however, the hotel, its residents, the porter, the faces glued on the room walls, the colorful stories, Shannon and the city were Mardi Gras itself.

Many years later, to my sadness, Shannon's words materialized in the form of a letter from Cuba. From my beloved *Papi...*

Chapter 9

La Habana

10 May

Mi querido hijo Nelson:

We received your letter today. We were so impatient with the delay. In fact, we were frantic when we heard the news on the radio about the Post Office airplanes suspending their flights between this country and the U.S. In these days of worries, the best and the only thing to do is to write letters, so it feels as if I were speaking to you and getting a lot off my chest.

Do you listen to the radio there? Any news about here? We've been living with the threat of an American invasion over our heads since Fidel took over. You know that, don't you, *hijo*?

Enriquito, your godson, is still the same. He comes here every day to play dominoes with me until eleven and sometimes he cleans all your records with alcohol. He complains that in your letters you never tell us when you are coming to visit. Enriquito has got this wonderful virtue: he does not forget you for a minute, Nelson. The other day, on TV, he thought that a handsome man on the screen was you and, out of the blue, he screamed, "Look! *Padrino* Nelson!"

Mamita asked me to tell you that she's ready to go to the U.S. and take care of your apartment, and any amount of money for her salary is fine with her. The problem, as you know, is that Blanco won't let her go. Well, how's she going to the U.S. if she can't -- like anybody else here -- get a passport and visa? Would she risk her life on the sea like so many have been doing all these years?

Gilda, your sister, keeps doing the same old things: sewing and embroidering the same kerchief and making flowers out of cloth, like Mimi. She has a new boyfriend, Renato. He seems to be a serious and decent man. Yesterday, they climbed into his red convertible Buick and disappeared into La Habana...

Well, *hijo*, the reason I'm writing this letter is certainly not a happy one. Don't panic, everybody is fine. The reason is a bit more disappointing and disheartening.

Do you remember the Castillo del Morro built by the Spaniards to defend themselves against the pirates at the port of La Habana? That's where all political prisoners, mentally ill and homosexuals have been taken, and eventually sent to either the camps or the fields. Yes, *hijo*, camps, which I never believed existed.... Until the day your Mother and I got this horrendous letter. Do you remember that Johnny and Juan spent months on end in the country a few years ago? We knew that they had been working in Pinar del Rio and that they had lost a lot of weight then. We even knew that it had to do with construction. But, *hijo*, your two brothers were actually working at the Castillo del Morro and were transferred to the country to help build the pavilions where those prisoners were to live.

When your Mother heard that from my own mouth -- I was reading the infamous letter -- she ran to the backyard as if she were looking for a safe place to be by herself. Since your Grandma died four years ago, that's where your Mother spends most of the her days now. My eyes were all teary, but I could see her, kneeling in the vegetable beds, sobbing. The soil was soaked by her tears.

She then lay down for a few minutes with her face in the dirt. Getting up, she had dust and rivulets of mud all over her face, and two big trails drawn by her own tears were running down her cheeks. She then grabbed the little hoe and started stabbing the ground as if by doing that she would get all her anger squeezed out of her. When I got closer to her, I heard a beautiful voice. It was your Mother, inexplicably singing *María Bonita*. Two feet away from her, I also started singing. When she turned around and saw me, I was scared at seeing her face in such state. Then she stood up and came over to me. We hugged, sang and cried. I know, I know, it sounds like an American musical you used to see at Cine Strand. We walked back towards our house in silence.

Late at night, in bed, I tried talking to her about it and she at once put her hand over my mouth, sealing my lips. Days have passed and we still have no courage to talk about it. Besides having to get used to this new way of life, which has quickly impoverished every single living and dead person on this island -- except those that belong to the Party -- we now have to face this under own roof. Finding out that your two older brothers have been working for this bloodthirsty and self-proclaimed government was as hard as an unexpected blow at our own faces. A government, which cannot, even stand by its own feet, and is always in need of billions of dollars from the Russians to go on existing. A government, which has forced its own people to leave their own houses to go to the fields and increase the production of sugar for some crazy economic plan. A government, which cannot even provide its people with the same sugar it produces. We are trapped!

And believe me, *hijo*, if there is someone who spends twenty-four hours a day praying for the end of these abnormalities, that person is me. What I most want at this moment is peace for all Cuban families.

I cannot go on writing, Nelson. Tears are welling up in my eyes now and I fear to smear these sheets of paper.

Affectionately, with much love from your...

Papi

Chapter 10

Years passed and life with Dino seemed to be the most perfect I could have ever imagined. I was doing pretty well in the real estate business and Dino, besides working at his father's construction company, wrote poetry at night.

On Saturdays, Dino used to go to the midtown Circulating Public Library. He would read for hours. Slowly, Dino started spending more time at the library. When I asked him why he was coming back home so late, he would languidly look at me and answer that he just could not stop reading. And I would believe him unconditionally. But he was doing that on a regular basis. I walked to the library to find out how late it was open on Saturdays. Yes, doubt had surreptitiously moved in my chest. And what I was told left me dumbfounded. The library closed at six in the evening!

Back home, I asked myself where Dino would go. He would silently come in, say a weak hello, and go to bed. Exhausted from being out so late the night before, he would then sleep all Sunday morning. He gradually stopped spending time with me and would go straight to his poems for the rest of the day. I didn't mind him writing endlessly to his muse, who, at that time, I thought it was me. I was wrong. I paced back and forth in the living room, trying to figure out what was going on with Dino.

A great heap of sadness possessed my heart then. I was confused. It was clear that Dino had some kind of problem. He was trying to hide it from me on purpose. A shadow seemed to have fallen on him. I looked for Dino in bed, and he would claim he was too tired. He seemed to be a stranger who was sharing the house with me, and grief was the only thing I could see in his eyes. I did not know what to do or say. Out of the blue, he was so cold and indifferent to me.

One Saturday afternoon, I followed him. Yes, I was playing the jealous housewife in some B-movie on TV in the wee hours. Dino left his office and walked to a bath house right in the middle of Fifty-sixth Street where he worked. On the one hand, I was shocked to see that Dino was not going to the library, as he had said, but, on the other hand, going to that place was a very good sign that he was trying to do something about his nerves and constant tiredness. Everybody knows the wonderful medicinal effects that steam baths have on a tired body. I bet you Dino went for a massage, a good masseur's fingers on your muscles can work miracles on you.

Silly Nelson.

Coming back home, I thought he would be more relaxed and grateful, but I was once enormously wrong. Dino said he was exhausted and he was going to bed early. When he was completely undressed, I noticed, on his left shoulder, a bluish bruise, magically in the shape of a rose. How had Dino gotten that tattoo? I tried to touch it, and as if he were a little boy jealous of his toys, for the first time since we had met, he yelled at me. I tried to plant little kisses on it and rub myself against his body, but Dino would not do a single thing. He stood still. Gently, I grabbed his hand and placed it on my dick and looked him in the eye. He blushed as usual, but his eyes were unreadable. He at once removed his hand as if my penis was burning it. And after an involuntary, old drag queen-like small shriek, I covered my mouth and ran out of the bedroom, sobbing. That night, I slept on the couch.

Things worsened between us. Dino closed an invisible door in my face and I just didn't know how to unlock it. I myself needed help. I was sinking. My parents were not writing me any longer, and I did not know what was going on in Cuba. I decided that time would bring not only Dino, but also *Papi's* letters to me. Then, one night, Dino kissed me good night, turned his back to me and quickly fell asleep. I started to toss in bed. When I couldn't stand the heat of his body near me anymore, I sat upright, turned the lamp on my nightstand and tried to read a book. Then I saw it. The little bluish rose had, like an amoeba, divided and given birth to lots of them, taking over Dino's back. I was frightened. I got up and trying not to make any noise, walked into the living room, opened the liquor closet, and poured myself a drink. I thought of the palm reader Shannon's predictions in New Orleans. What was that? I was a nervous wreck. I walked back and forth in the living room like a drunken cockroach till daybreak.

I left our apartment in Brooklyn for a few days

by the sea. When I came back, Dino had already gone, without leaving a single note. A few days later, I found out that he had moved to San Francisco, where his family was living at that time. He eventually worked at their Laundromat in the Castro District. The great thing about their store was that they played opera records for their customers. I kept picturing their illegal, green-cardless Chinese employees ironing clothes and rolling up pairs of socks to the rhythms of La Bohème, listening to Mimi's frail voice and Rodolfo's bursts of jealousy.

One January morning, I unexpectedly received a call from Dino's brother, Jackie, who cried while he talked to me. Dino's blue roses had taken over his whole body. It was as if the stems of his blue roses had gotten tangled up in such way on his back that there was no space left, clogging up his weakened lungs. Oh, Dino, how blind and insensitive I must have seemed. I tried to reach out for you, but you wouldn't let me. Then, someone or something up there chose for you the way you could love me better: from the distance, from beyond the clouds.

Chapter 11

La Habana

7 September

Nelson:

Today we did not receive a letter from you, but a skinny, black box and a long letter from Pepe's family. What we have to tell you is certainly not good news. What was inside that box, I shall let you know in a minute. Be patient.

I have no idea if you have ever realized that you never received a single line from Pepe himself. The reason for that is very simple: he was arrested a couple of years ago and sent immediately to a concentration camp. They found out that he was a homosexual through an *informante*, the kind of people that populate the island now. I have never been to hell, I think, but living here feels just like it: little devils reporting to their superior demons twenty-four hours a day. Sorry if I have to use all these metaphors, but I am afraid this letter may be intercepted and read by those fallen angels out there.

Getting back to your friend... Pepe was sent to one of those concentration camps (in Cuba?), which I believe should be burned as soon as possible. He and all those young men and women had to go there and once in the fields, cut down sugar cane stalks for ten or twelve hours a day, plus suffer rituals of kicks and rifle butts against their faces. I haven't the faintest idea how his family got to know about it, but it seems that the only pastime those young men had was -- when the green-uniformed men were not around -- sprinkling a few drops of water on their faces and then some sugar so that they would look they all of a sudden were wearing makeup and with pieces of charcoal from the burned cane stalks in the fields, they would paint around their eyes and put on skirts made out of potato sacks and old bed sheets. Can you imagine that? Nobody can, Nelson. And this is how the box that his family sent us this morning comes into the story.

Pepe somehow, while his apartment was being searched, begged the green-complexioned men if he could bring some of his records. Miraculously, they allowed him to bring only one. And Pepe took the box of *La Forza Del Destino* along. The record player? A friend of his had smuggled one inside the camp. And that's how they spent a few hours, listening to the record you once sold him.

And today, we got the box back. Inside, we found the set of records all smashed as if it had been hammered into a thousand little pieces. And at the bottom of it was a letter addressed to you. It said that at the moment he was writing, he was sitting under the shade of a spreading tree, staring off into space and thinking fondly of you. He was also happy that you had left for the United States in time. He did not wish his worst enemy to experience what he was going through, then. Reminiscing about when you two used to go from bar to bar in La Habana, he described, in detail, one night that you two were at *El Carmelo* and flirted with a young American man called Walter.

I could not continue reading. My glasses fell in my lap and my eyes fogged up. My head felt like it had water inside. Heavy. You Mother and I could not believe his words. We hugged and stayed there, rocking each other. Your Mother wanted to burn the box and the letter at once. I said no. It took us a few days to finish reading it. When your Mother and I were almost getting into swing of things, trying to find in our hearts some comfort and peace, after we found out about your brothers Johnny and Juan, we got this second disturbing and worst piece of news these two old folks have ever received.

Finding out that you are a homosexual, a *maricón*, was more painful than seeing Cuba being raped by those demons out there. Why, Nelson? I have missed you every single day after you left so many years ago. Almost eighteen. This empty vacuum that you left behind has never been filled by anyone. I keep thinking of when you shaved and sang at the same time. I keep thinking of when you craved baby food when I had prepared so exquisite dishes in my now empty kitchen.

Your Mother came down with fever and I had to call the pharmacist, who did not charge a nickel. I guess that's what they call free healthcare. Hah! She is feeling much better now and went back to gardening and planting in the kitchen garden every morning. As a matter of fact, I can hear her beauty-ful voice singing now.

We, two old people, who have always lived our

lives with dignity, are forced to face two other tragedies by our own offspring. Finding out all these things about you through a letter written by someone else is extremely disappointing and sad. Why didn't you ever tell me, Nelson? Even if I do not agree with the person you seem to be... you are... Why didn't you ever confide in me, *hijo*? We spent hours on end in your bedroom talking about life and operas? Why didn't you tell me, Nelson? It really feels as if I was then with a stranger and that's what it hurts me the most.

We would like to ask you not to wait for our letters for a while. We need some time to think and talk all about this. We need time for ourselves. We need peace.

Brokenhearted, I say *adios* for now...

Papi & Mami

P.S. -- *Mamita is the only one here who says she will always be on your side. She says she loves you too much not to understand you.*

Chapter 12

When the airplane was landing, I looked through the window and saw Rio. Magically located at the Guanabara Bay, I could see the mountains, the shantytowns, the Atlantic Ocean, the open sea... For a split second, my beloved Havana came to mind. I had always wanted to come down to Rio ever since I was a kid. Although I was not at a very good phase in my life, after all I had gone through with Dino and *Papi*'s letters, Rio seemed to be the right place for me to be then. I wanted to enjoy my vacation in peace so much.

I took a taxi to Copacabana and Silvia was in the lobby, waiting for me. Silvia was Gil's maid. Gil, the person from whom I had rented the apartment, was a delicious, middle-aged, and toned man. He was drying his hair with the thickest towel I had ever seen in my life when I stepped into the apartment. He had just come back from the beach, four blocks from the building. The apartment had no stove; it was not hooked up because Gil was then selling it. He invited me to stay at his place, but I decided to stay in the empty apartment by myself.

On the following day, I woke up around 8. Why? I was on vacation, wasn't it? Gil called around 10 and wanted to introduce me to his friends. I said I would like to go to the beach by myself instead. And off I went. I saw a group of young men fighting and dancing to the rhythms of drums. I thought they were rehearsing for *Carnaval*, but I was then told they were doing *Capoeira*, a martial art created by the slaves in Brazil. They all had tight bodies. All muscles. And unabashedly sexy. They were wearing loose white pants, whose legs were cut short. Their bulges jutted out as far as one could imagine. And I got nervous, short of breath actually. Their over-tanned skin sparkled in the sun. Their dark skin contrasted with the white, fine sand on the ground. A man kept flirting with me while I was watching those kids flying over our heads.

On my third day in Rio, the day was beautiful. On my way to the beach, I stopped by a bookstore and bought a book by Argentinian author Julio Cortázar. I was on page 22 of my book, where, according to Cortázar ants are certainly bound to eat Rome up, when I felt a cold, wet hand on my left shoulder. There he was, the man who I had been flirting with the day before. He was standing in front of me, and dripping. His crotch was right in my face. I had to shade my eyes to see him better. I asked him to please take a seat next to me. I noticed he was wearing a gold bracelet on his left wrist. He had a nice body and a bushy blond mustache. His eyes matched the blue-green Copacabana sea that embraced the shore before us. He was a hunk, indeed. His trunks were quite short and revealed his bikini line. I at once asked him if he wanted a cig. He said he'd take one after he got his hands dried on my thick beach towel. I had borrowed the same one Gil was using when we first met. I immediately did a gig based on the movie *Now Voyager*, the part that Paul Henreid manages to tuck two cigarettes between his fingers, bring both of them to his mouth, light them at the same time and hand one to Bette Davis. The movie amazingly has some of its scenes shot in Rio (actually they used that old trick of projecting the setting behind the characters on the wall), where Bette comes down for a rest. Yeah, right! A little embarrassed, the hunk accepted the cigarette and then took a long drag, savoring it. Ten minutes was the time we took to go from the beach to my apartment.

Soon, I was rolling up two cigs with local marijuana, generously left by Gil. This time, the hunk grabbed my hand, took hold of the cigs, lit them by imitating me at the beach. Stoned, we zigzagged our way to the open-aired servant's area, past the kitchen, and kept looking at a beautiful sunset behind the hills with their balancing shacks.

We kissed the longest kiss. Boy, were we horny! Going back to the empty living room, I asked him to take his trunks off. I started to shake and went to the bathroom cabinet to get a bottle of baby lotion. I started rubbing some on his legs and feet. We embraced. I said I wanted to rub some on his back and we went to the bedroom. I licked his ears. I massaged his whole body, wanting him so badly; I missed the body a man so much. He then said, "Stand up and turn around, Nelson." I saw him firmly squeezing the pink lotion onto his fingers, and the next thing I remember was that at midnight, side by side, we were awakened by the sounds of samba drums downstairs.

***

I was taking a nap when the doorbell awakened me. It was the *girls*, Gil's friends, bringing our costumes for the ball. Yes, Gil had talked me into joining them. We were a group of eight girls, excited to shake our booties in some *Carnaval* ball all night long. We had a simple and inexpensive costume: we would all dress like bumble bees. We were to wear black leotards and strap two little pillows, stuffed with cotton balls, and a spiral-like design on them, to our hinies, one for each cheek. On our heads, *Brillo* pads, imitating hair with long antennae made out of drinking straws and small fluorescent green foam balls glued to the top of them. And gigantic boobs, of course. And high-heeled shoes, preferably Cuban heels, of course. And kilos of makeup, of course. We were *The erotic bees, of course!* And here they were, trying on the costumes in the empty apartment, whose living room was transformed into a runway in seconds. Mario, one of Gil's friends who were trying to make it in the theater scene in Rio, brought a portable sewing machine for the last touches. The *Brillo* pads on our heads looked hilarious. Soon, we were all stoned and happy, drinking *caipirinhas* and smoking marijuana. They all left only after eating three huge pizza pies we ordered from the pizza place on the corner. They all almost ate the young delivery boy first.

Two days later, *Carnaval* was in the air. Every building in the neighborhood had something that reminded you of *Carnaval*: streamers, balloons, papers stars. People wore costumes and heavy theatrical makeup even during the day. Especially the children. You could see little fairies (let alone the big ones!), boy soldiers, hoodlums, princesses, frogs, pirates, bearded girls coming down the hills or walking up the streets. Confetti and streamers littered everywhere.

And the Erotic bees, inside a rented VW van, drove to the Gay Ball. Gil had the tickets under his *Brillo* wig. I couldn't stop laughing. People unashamedly checked us out. We got into the club and I thought I had stepped into another world. The room was smoke-filled, reminding me of any gay bar in New York. Sequined fairies, mustached men in delicate laced wedding gowns, muscular boys wearing almost nothing, queens in queen's beaded garment, old men with ostrich feathers on their heads. The music was typical Brazilian *Carnaval* songs. Very loudly. People kissed in a dark corner of the room. And sweat... and beer drinking... and music... and kisses... and more sweat and more beer. And more beer... and *caipirinhas*...

Of course, Gil drove me to Corcovado, then the Sugar Loaf and then to the Samba Schools parade with thousands of people dancing on this long avenue, downtown Rio. For two weeks I was swept by an avalanche of food, drink and sex. Almost nonstop. Until the day I decided to go to the beach by myself when and where I had another turning point in my life.

The sun was scalding by one. I was people watching when Gil showed up at the beach bringing some friends of his along. I then got up and decided to swim. The water felt good, and it was the bluest one you could imagine. As I was going into the water, a Brazilian god suddenly walked by me. While I was jumping over the rough waves, he seemed to walk through them so easily. I looked at him and he looked back at me. I swear we two felt a current, an electric shock that came from him to me and vice versa. I started feeling the water warmer and he stayed there three feet from me, motionless. He was getting closer and closer. I was shaking. He looked me in the eye and pointed to the beach. Then, he left.

I took a dive immediately. My heart throbbed. My dick throbbed. Underwater, I thought to myself: What's going on, Nelson? Who's this kid with the most wonderful body in those sensual short trunks? Because of its white color, it was transparent when it was wet and I could see his dick all right. How can I describe it? It was... godly!

When I got out of the water, the Brazilian god was lying on his beach towel near the beer and shrimp stand. While drying myself off, I picked up the glass of *caipirinha* on the sand, took a sip and kept looking at him. Then, I saw something I never forgot: one his balls uninhibitedly was coming out of his trunks. I choked on a piece of lime I was chewing. I had to drink something to wash it down. Gil noticed I was choking and came to pat me on the back. I felt relieved and better when I finally swallowed the lime. Then, the Brazilian god got up and came towards me slowly. He walked like a cat, I swear. I was sitting and trying to dry myself. Standing near me, his body looked even more perfect. He was in his twenties.

"Hi," he said.

"Hi. Care for a drink?"

He turned it down. He said he did not drink. Smoke? No, he did not smoke, either. I guess he was not used to earthly, mundane vices! After all, he was a god. I could not stop looking at his crotch. And he noticed it. He then sat down and started asking me a few questions, like where I was from, if I liked *Carnaval*, how long I was going to stay in Rio. I thought he was trying to pick me up, a male hooker. I was damn wrong. This turned out to be the sweetest thing to happen to me in Rio. Meeting the way we did felt like watching the Samba Schools or the Gay ball with the Erotic bees. It was an unforgettable feeling. Something one cannot experience twice.

His name was Carlos. I introduced him to everybody around and to our surprise, he said, "I practice *Capoeira* here on the beach." And, out of the blue, he started dancing, cart-wheeling and kicking at the air. And I fell in love.

I asked Carlos if he wanted to come to my apartment for a drink. He said he couldn't because he had to go to work at six. He took care of the Portuguese consul's mansion in Barra, a distant beach neighborhood in the south of Rio. He said that he could come over the following day, though, because it was his day off. On a paper napkin, I scribbled my address and phone number. Before Carlos left for work, Gil took a picture of us: he puts his hand on my left shoulder and I put my arm around his waist. The sea is in the background. Blue and white waves spit frothy and salty water on the shore, at our feet.

Gil winked at me approvingly.

Chapter 13

Bringing Carlos to the United States turned out to be idealistic and complicated. Sure I had to give him some credit for no sooner had we arrived, than he enrolled in a language school near our apartment in Brooklyn. We were living in a beautiful, roomy garden apartment. I found him a job: he cleaned the houses of a few friends of mine, making good pocket money with which he paid part of his evening Photography classes. A dream he said he had always had when he lived in Brazil.

"I have to, Carlos."

"Of course, you don't have to, Nelson."

"Are you jealous again?"

"What d'you think?"

"C'mon. You know I love only you; otherwise, I wouldn't have brought you from Brazil. We've gone through that so many times, hon."

"And how many times are you going to repeat

that you brought me here, *hon*?"

"Till you understand that there's no other person in my life, but you silly."

"I still think you want to open that bar to be close to those... *kids*."

"Stop it. You know, I also have reasons to suspect you, Carlos. You spend most of time outside this apartment now. How many houses have you been cleaning lately?"

"Five."

"And how many of them have only one man living there?"

"Shut up."

"See? *You* can be jealous of me and *I* can't be jealous of you. Not fair."

"You brought me here."

"Now, *you*'re bringing that up again."

"I just think you should try selling more houses. That's all."

"Yes, but I've always dreamed of having a disco-piano-bar, Carlos. And *Sal's* can be that dream come true. Salvatore, the owner, is not asking a lot, just enough for him to keep it. And I have the money. It's a great opportunity."

"I still think..."

"You've done your homework?"

"Huh?"

"Carlos, stop dancing and swinging your hips that way and tell me: have you finished your homework?"

"Nelson, I'm not dancing. I am practicing *Capoeira*."

"Stand still, please. You haven't answered my question."

"Yes?"

"Are you using your English outside the classroom?"

"I am. Why?"

"A few friends of mine have told me that you keep avoiding them. Is that because you don't like them or because you can't speak the language?"

"Both."

"But if you want to stay in this country, you've got to speak English."

"And to stay I also need my documents, right?"

"I know. I've talked to a friend of mine and she's willing to marry you."

"Really? Will I have to..."

"Of course not, you silly. She's a *dyke*."

"Good. When can we get married?"

"She told me as soon as she closes this big deal. She's trying to sell that building on Court and Bergen Streets."

"Tell her I'm ready."

"Look who's in a hurry to get married now!"

"Yes, but it's a fake marriage, isn't it? Just for my green card."

"And what are you going to do when you get it?"

"Don't know yet."

"You can go outside the U.S. with it."

"Yes. Bob told me."

"Who's Bob?"

"The guy whose house I clean on Thursdays."

"You've talked to him about your legal status in this country?"

"In plain, good Portuguese. His Brazilian ex-lover taught him."

"And what else do you talk to him about?"

"You're jealous, Nelson."

"It's just a simple question. Can't you answer me?"

"I can hear it in your voice. You're burning up with jealousy."

"Carlos, *please...*"

"I want to teach, Nelson."

"But what?"

"*Capoeira*."

"I know but you need to speak English well to explain it to your students."

"I'll try."

"Fine, So find a place to teach and I will see what I can do."

I had said that in the hope that he would never find a place and consequently his dream would fade in a matter of days. I was wrong. Two weeks later, Carlos found a gym and talked the owner -- I don't know how -- into letting him teach the famous Brazilian martial art.

I now felt it was my turn: my own disco-piano-bar was just seven blocks away from our apartment. One day, the owner, Salvatore, an old, butchy queen, who wore a button in the shape of two pink little hands on his lapel, proposed partnership to me. I simply could not say no to my dream right before my eyes.

I then decided to go on with it, eventually I would convince Carlos that I also had dreams. I walked down to *Sal's* and looked at the building across from the street. I was in love with the idea of having my own bar. The sidewalks were empty. It was a mildly cold day, around six in the evening. I saw that the red and blue neon sign hanging at the entrance, poor thing, was in deplorable state. The upper half of the first "S" was unlit. Looking a bit harder, something else also bothered my eyes: the lower half of the second "S" was burned out. I thought that if I didn't do anything urgent to the bar, it would sink as soon as I could say yes to Sal. I took a deep breath and walked into the bar.

It was dark inside, but still not filled with cigarette smoke, since it was too early for the crowd of *girls* to show up. Sal was in his office. The door was ajar and when I pushed it open, he was sitting behind a very small jacaranda desk. Behind him were posters of old silent movies and an immense framed blue and green butterfly pinned upon a white background. There was a big stuffed frog on one of the shelves, where Sal also stored magazines, books and all kinds of porno movies. While I talked to him, I had the impression that that frog would hop into my lap at any moment.

"Hi, Sal."

"How're you doing, Nelson? Hope you're bringing me good news."

"Maybe."

"Do you want to talk more about it?"

"Yes. I've been thinking. Sal, I'll be very honest with you. I still cannot stop working with the real estate business and dedicate myself entirely to the bar. I was..."

"I know what you want to say. Of course, I agree with you. I'll be taking care of it. I never told you I wanted to leave *Sal's*. I said I needed a partner to come in with cash so that I could keep my doors open. That's all."

"So it means I won't have to be here most of the time?"

"Of course not."

"There's one more thing, Sal."

"Tell me, *child.*"

"I want to be in charge of the shows. Listen, I have lots of ideas..."

"Sure. You know very well how tired I am to deal with all those drag queens and their big egos out there. Go ahead. Be my guest."

"Then..."

"Deal?"

"Yes."

'Let me shake your hand, *pardner.*"

"There, partner."

Sal tenderly grabbed my neck, missed my cheek and kissed my left ear as if to seal our agreement. Then I left his office a bit deaf because of his kiss. On my way out, I noticed that three monitors hanging from the ceiling were already on showing the faces of two beautiful, lanky, sun-tanned boys, kissing.

On the sidewalk, I lifted my eyes and looked straight at the neon sign and miraculously, both "S's" were lit as if they were welcoming my joining the bar. I took that as a sign of good luck. Then, I literally flew back home.

***

"You what?"

"I'm taking the money out the bank tomorrow to close the business with Sal."

"I don't believe you, Nelson."

"This can be my meal ticket out of the uncertain real estate business."

"Really?"

"Why are you reacting that way, Carlos? I really expected you to support me on this."

"I have a feeling that this is not going to be a good thing. I'm sorry, Nelson."

"Is it asking too much of you to be on my side?"

"No, Nelson, but a disco-piano-bar? I've thought you were an experienced businessman. I guess I was wrong. Can't you see this is just a temporary fad?"

"Right. But as long as is, we can make lots of money out of it. Besides, I've always wanted to be in show biz. This can be a start."

"Dream on, *hon.*"

"I see it won't be easy to convince you. Are you helping me or what?"

"What could I do?"

"First, you could help me clean and paint the office and once that job is over, be our bouncer, since you're so strong and a *Capoeira* fighter."

"You're kidding?"

"We'd pay you, of course."

"D'you really think I'd be able to be standing at your bar in the wee hours after having scrubbed and cleaned all those houses during the day?"

"You could quit a couple."

"No way."

"Would you think about it, please?"

"Ok, then."

He did think about it. Five minutes later, he came out of the bathroom, telling me that he didn't even want to be near the bar. Fine, I thought, I don't need your help.

***

The deal was done and I wanted to celebrate. I called Diego, a friend who owned an antique store, and told him about the bar. Diego said that we should then go and face the dance floor at *Sal's*. He would bring his lover Dan along too.

Carlos did not show any enthusiasm but, to my surprise, did not decline the invitation, either. We were there in less than ten minutes.

It was crowded and you could smell the cigarette smoke three blocks away. Carlos did not want to go into the office with me, but I needed to see Sal. Carlos stayed in the bar's mid-sized front room where three pinball machines made everybody blind and deaf. Carlos was a pinball wiz when he lived in Rio.

Beauties and more beauties shook their groove

things to the sound of Gloria Gaynor's hit *I Will Survive*. In unison, and very loudly, they all sang that they should have changed that stupid lock and made their lovers leave their keys. And I laughed my head off.

After talking to Sal, who was more drunk than a gay fish, I came out to check on Carlos who wouldn't stop punching the buttons on the sides of the pinball machines.

When I went back to the dance floor, a blond hunk, with a three-day stubble, started giving me the eye. My heart raced. I hadn't felt that since I met Carlos at the beach in Rio more than six months then. I unashamedly responded to his lusty eyes. Approaching, he handed me his glass of gin tonic. I had always hated that drink, but I accepted it, taking a tiny sip. We started chatting. Only then had I noticed he was a bit too high and a bit too close to my face. He grabbed me by the waist and kissed me. I had no time to avoid it. The kid was in heat. At this very moment with a big winning smile on his face, over the blond hunk's shoulder, I saw who I wanted to see the least in the entire world: Carlos's face froze when our eyes met. And I froze in fear. Carlos stayed there for a few seconds. The only thing that crossed my mind was that had Carlos lost the pinball game that night, he would have killed the blond hunk in heat using his *Capoeira* kicks in two seconds.

Carlos didn't, though. He rushed out of the bar without looking back. Diego had been watching everything from one corner of the bar and came over to me as soon as Carlos had left.

"Nelson, let'im go. Everything will be fine when you get home."

"I'm not that certain."

"What do you think he's going to do? Pack his things and move?"

"Carlos is pigheaded and he may as well do that."

"Where's he going to go?"

"I don't know, Diego. New York is pretty big."

"What's going on, Nelson? Would you like to talk?"

"I don't know if I should."

"C'mon. We've been friends for many years. Get it off your chest, child."

"I feel Carlos is longing for Brazil, and I don't know what else I can do for him to adapt to his new life here."

"Give him some time. Aren't you pushing him too much? Listen, when we all came to this country, we also had to go through so many things, remember?"

"Maybe you're right, Diego. I've got to let Carlos do things the way he wants for a while.

***

Wrong. When Diego, Dan and I got back home about four in the morning -- we shared a taxi and before he left, I had invited them for a last nightcap -- I thought I had just entered the stage of a studio where a very sugary, extremely melodramatic Latin soap opera was being filmed at that very moment. I turned the key and unlocked the door.

There was something blocking it. I thought that the big earthenware vase had fallen right behind it. I pushed it harder and the door suddenly surrendered. Guess what -- or who -- was right on the floor, lying on the rug blocking the entrance? Right. Him. Half consciously, Carlos had foamy vomit coming out of his mouth. Of course I got scared. He had definitely tried committing suicide in my house. We two carried him by his arms and legs and immediately threw him fully dressed in the bathtub. I turned on the shower and, while he repeated my name and some silly line like *Oh, my life is finished,* Carlos received the coldest jets of water ever. Instinctively, he opened his big green eyes wide and jumped out of the bathtub like a scared cat. But we wouldn't let him go that easily and pushed him back in, holding him down for a couple of minutes.

Undressing Carlos in our bedroom, Diego and I dried him and put him to bed right away. Still calling my name as if he were a frail, young girl dying of some disease of the lung and opening his eyes as if to recognize where he was, we left him alone in the room. I went into the kitchen to make Carlos some chamomile tea. At least that was the only kind of tea that had crossed my mind. Dan, coming back out of the bathroom, walked into the kitchen to show me a couple of plastic bottles of sleeping pills and aspirin that were floating in the washbasin water in the bathroom. Apparently, that was what Carlos had swallowed to take his life. Yeah, right! When my friend left, I opened the sofabed in the living room and got ready to go to sleep. But first, I went back to the bedroom to give

Carlos a cup of the tea. On the sofabed, before falling asleep, I lay there thinking for a while: yes, I was undoubtedly very mad at Carlos for doing that to him and to me on that unforgettable night.

***

"I saw it, Carlos."

"What did you see, Nelson?"

"You and Bob making out on his sofa."

"How?"

"Through his living room window."

"I can't believe you did that, Nelson. You had no right to do that."

"What was I supposed to think? You spend most of the time there. Don't tell me you've been cleaning his house every single day?"

"Bob's become a good friend. That's all."

"That only?"

At this moment, Carlos got infuriated, walked out of our bedroom and went straight to our living room. Suddenly I heard the sound of glasses being smashed. Carlos had kicked the tall reproduction of an eighteenth century golden framed mirror that I had bought at Diego's antique shop years before.

Blood squirted out of his toes really badly. I then tried to help him, but he wouldn't let me. He was furious. I had never seen him like that; he looked like a caged animal. He didn't want me to get near him. And I was afraid of his using *Capoeira* fatal kicks on me.

"I feel like killing you right now, Nelson. How could you do that?"

"Carlos, I... don't... trust you anymore."

"I hate you, Nelson. I hate you for bringing me to this country. I hate you for finding me this kind of job. I hate your bar. I hate you for spying on me. I hate you!"

The trust I had in a lover was once again broken. And that fight took place exactly seven months after Carlos had tried his fake suicide. I loved him so much, but at the same time, I just did not know what to do for him to feel at home. Brazil was on his mind twenty-four hours a day, and the only thing that made him happy was his *Capoeira* classes. Fortunately, his English was improving fast.

"Where are you going, Carlos?"

"None of your business."

"Oh, yes?"

Now, *I* was furious. Opening his chest of

drawers, I started picking up all his clothes and threw them out of our bedroom window right onto the street. He looked even angrier, but he did not do anything aggressive. He left the apartment, slamming the door behind him. I watched him from the window collecting his clothes and stuffing them in a suitcase he had taken from the closet.

***

"Nelson, what's going on?" asked Diego on the other side of the line.

"Is Carlos over there with you?"

"I can't talk."

"I got it. He is there. I can't take this anymore, Diego. I'm sending him back to Brazil as soon as I can."

"Nelson, it seems that that's what he wants also."

"Great. How's his foot?"

"It's stopped bleeding. I'm taking him to the pharmacy on the corner, though."

"Thanks, Diego. I've got to go now."

"Nelson, whatever happens, I just want the best for you two."

Carlos had finally done something sensible: he was with our friend Diego. Myself, I was trembling from head to toe. I then poured a drink and chain-smoked. Half an hour later, I dialed the Brazilian airlines office in Manhattan.

"Good afternoon. Varig."

"I need to go to Brazil tomorrow. This is an emergency case. My mother's just passed away in Brazil."

"I'm sorry to hear that, sir."

"Thank you."

"Yes. There's a seat on the flight tomorrow leaving from JFK at ten p.m. You should be there by eight. Would you care to make the reservation now?"

"Yes. The sooner the better."

"Your name, please?"

"Carlos Santos. When can I get the ticket?"

"I can send it by messenger right away."

"Wonderful."

Twenty minutes later, I called Diego back to tell him the news. I asked him to stop by the house to pick up the airplane ticket for Carlos, since I didn't want to see his face again. On the following evening, Carlos returned to his beloved Brazil.

Chapter 14

When I first came to work at the bar, Salvatore gave me *carte blanche* to do whatever I pleased. My first plan was to do something innovating: I wanted to change the stereotypical image of a gay bar. We were at the beginning of the eighties and I knew very well that it wouldn't be easy. All those queens had been pretty much conditioned to the same kind of bar for years all over the city, the country and, who knows, the planet. But instead of dark, smoke and stale-smelling, I wanted it to be more like a music hall-disco-piano-bar. I wanted jazz singers with their hoarse voices at happy hour in the evening but, of course, drag queens wearing canary-yellow costumes, gold-lame belts and lots of white feathers on their heads performing their gig late into the night. I wanted to keep the pinball machines at the entrance as well as the TV monitors hanging on the ceiling; however, porno videos only in the wee hours.

And what I really wanted to introduce to the regulars was opera. That's right. I know a lot of people associate opera with gay men, but that's not quite true. There are great numbers of them who have never heard of Puccini or Wagner. That became exactly my personal touch to the bar. Opera on the hanging monitors. Sal almost fell off his chair when I told him about it. He was afraid of losing his clientele the moment they saw some voluptuous, sweaty, bearded man screaming at their ears instead of those cute, lean, blond boys moaning and groaning in any porno movie. Although, according to our agreement, now Sal could not go back to what he said to me once I had given him the money. He almost fell off his chair again when, one day, I brought an artist friend to paint both restrooms. Sal at first thought that my friend was to give a fresh coat of paint on the walls, but that was not what happened. On the men's room ceiling, I had him paint the scene from La Bohème where Mimi is coughing incessantly while her beloved Rodolfo is asleep inside a bar. In the women's room, another scene of La Bohème: pale and terribly ill, Mimi is dying in bed, surrounded by her closest friends while Rodolfo sobs in a corner of the room.

The opening day. Before going to check on the girls in the dressing room, I stopped by the bar and ordered a double whiskey on the rocks. Besides being nervous, I was drinking quite heavily since Carlos had left the United States. I had been alone in the apartment for six months.

The girls that night were not going to do their usual lip-synching of Diana, Judy or Barbra. They were going to premiere a new number: a spoof of La Bohème. However, the fellow queen who was going to play Marcello had come down with the flu and I was to sub for him at the last minute. For two weeks I had been directing the piece. I wore a white leotard and to both my embarrassment and delight, my crotch jutted out as far as one can imagine. It didn't matter to me since by ten I was very high on drinks and two miniature marijuana roaches I had brought from home. The show was scheduled for eleven.

Minutes before we started, I peeked from behind an improvised curtain in back of the stage and saw my friends in the audience. Diego and Dan were sitting right on the second row. We had a good audience that night, for it was the end of summer and the local biweekly Brooklyn's Cobble Hill newspaper had run an ad on both our bar and show.

With the first chords, the needle on the record produced the scratchy sound which to me meant opera. Seconds later we were on stage. Most of the audience, of course, did not understand a word we were lip-synching.

In the plot, the philosopher and the musician started to argue. They pretended to arm themselves with imaginary swords. As they dueled, the painter and the poet laughed. The audience was also laughing their heads off, since it looked ridiculous watching four old queens in leotards, wearing heavy theatrical makeup, doing a very cheap spoof of one of the greatest operas ever composed.

We gyrated and gyrated and flying off the stage, we fell right onto the first row. The music was louder by then. Seeing that the duelists were becoming more infuriated by the second, the poet, as if he could read their minds and changing the opera radically, in an attempt to save me, grabbed my crotch at the exact moment the two duelists were to stab it. I screamed, finishing the act on a high-pitched note. The curtain came down and the audience burst into laughter.

"Congratulations. I never knew you could act," said a voice behind me.

Before I turned around in my chair, like a ghost from my past, I saw his face reflected in the mirror that I looked myself. With a little cotton ball, I was taking the makeup off very carefully so that I wouldn't have my mustache smeared with it.

"Ronald! Oh, my... Oh, my...What a surprise."

"And look who's here with me."

"Walter!"

"In the flesh, honey."

"We're so happy for you, Nelson," Ronald said. And while taking my hands, he added, "These are still cold, huh?"

"When did you come in?"

"We saw the whole number. We didn't miss a second, honey," Walter answered with a big smile on his face.

"Did you like it?"

"Liked it? We loved it, child."

Diego and Dan marched into the dressing room minutes later. Hugging me, they handed me a bouquet of flowers. Afterwards, we went for drinks at our bar. I still couldn't believe Walter and Ronald were there with me. Years and years passed since we had last seen one another. At three-thirty, we left *Sal's*. I suggested that we walk so that we would have more time to chat and gossip. The streets of Brooklyn at the time were not as dangerous and the sky was full of stars. At my door, I asked them to come in for a Cuban espresso, but they declined, claiming it was too late and they had to get a cab back to the City. After Walter and Ronald wrote down their telephone numbers, I entered my apartment. Locking the door, I walked towards the TV and turned it on right away. I then realized that I was helplessly alone.

***

The door bell rang three times. My eyelids did not feel like opening. With difficulty, I focused on the alarm clock on the nightstand. It read nine o'clock. Cursing whomever was there, I got out of bed, naked. Wrapping myself in the bed sheet, I opened the door a crack and saw a ConEd man.

"Morning. Need to come in to read the meter."

"Sure."

Wearing an extremely pressed on dark blue uniform, his blond, hairy arms turned me on immediately. Lying to him that the meter was in my bedroom (how could he have fallen for that?), I let the bed sheet slide my body down to the floor. Surprised, he followed me…

***

The firehouse was right across from my apartment. Once in a while, their siren and truck lights invaded and inundated my living room with its lush bright red light. Sometimes, I would spread the curtain apart and watch them coiling and uncoiling those thick hoses, which certainly turned me on. Craning my neck out of the living room window, I always hoped to see some unusual and mainly sexual affairs going on in there. I heard that the firemen had brought two ladies of the night inside the building once.

"What happened, Mr. Nelson?"

"I think my basement is on fire."

"Seriously? I'll go and call the others."

"No, no. Maybe we two could go down and check first? No need to alarm them now."

"I can't see anything in here."

Good, I thought to myself.

"It's pretty dark. I wish I had brought my flashlight."

"You have, hon. It's right here," I said reaching for his crotch.

"Mr. Nelson!"

That was all he moaned and I used his "flashlight" in the dark of the basement for a quite long time.

***

"Nelson, would you please stop it?" asked Sal.

"What?"

"Gosh. You're my partner now. I don't think you should be doing that..."

"Listen, pal..."

"Who's this now?"

"Sal, I want you to meet..."

"I don't want to meet anybody. Look at yourself, Nelson. I thought you'd said you wanted us to change the image of the bar."

"I do."

"But you're acting as if you didn't want to."

"Listen, pal…"

"You shut the hell up."

I had to do something before Sal kicked the beauty I had found that night at the bar. About twenty something, the tall green-eyed boy was about to start a fight with Sal. But I took his arm and pulled him out of the bar to the street. We walked to my apartment where we later made love all over the place.

***

The doorbell rang four times. Nine-thirty. I cursed whomever was at the door.

"Registered letter."

"So?"

"I need you to sign this slip."

Peter was the mail carrier whom, for the longest time, I had a crush on. I couldn't let him get away.

"Want some coffee?"

"I can't…"

I could hear in his voice that he sure wanted some. Now it was a matter of insisting a little bit.

'C'mon, it won't take long."

"All right, then."

"Please, sit down, Pete."

"I see the letter comes from Brazil," he shouted from the living room.

I was in the kitchen, looking for the espresso coffeepot. Rummaging through the drawer where I kept the silverware, I had absolutely no idea what he was doing in the living room.

"Oh, Brazil? Didn't even notice," I shouted back.

"Y'know anybody there?"

Finally finding the coffee under the sink, I said yes to his question and unwillingly dropped the can, whose plastic lid opened, spilling the powder all over the floor. Then, kneeling by the sink, out of the blue, I saw two naked feet next to my hand, which moved quickly to clean the mess I had made. When I lifted my eyes, I unexpectedly saw Peter massaging and stroking his penis right in my face, in my kitchen. Three minutes later, on high flame, the espresso coffeepot started whistling on the stove.

***

It was Diego's birthday and he had invited all

the *girls* to his apartment for a small get-together. Soon Diego came to me and whispered in my ear that he was carrying on with this beauty who had also brought his boyfriend along to the party. I myself was interested in another beauty who said he was from the Bronx. A Latino hunk. He wore a well-kept mustache, just like mine. Diego's stereo kept playing disco and salsa, merengue and rumba. The party was over by three in the morning because of the annoying threats his old lady neighbor was making to call the police.

"I don't, Diego. I never liked group sex."

"Ok, then, I'll go with the two boys, plus Dan, to my room and you stay here with your cutie."

"Perfect."

Ten minutes later, Diego showed up in the living room, stark naked, imploring, "Nelson, please come help me. Just can't do it with these two hunks and they are too beautiful for me to let'em go."

Next, Diego, the Latino hunk and I entered the bedroom to find the two other boys and Dan sound asleep.

***

"What's going on, Nelson?"

"What d'you mean, Sal?"

"Lately, you've only come in to check the cash register."

"Not true. What're you trying to imply, Sal? That I'm stealing from you?

"I never said that."

"Well, what did you call me for?"

"Nelson, I really see you as a good friend."

I looked at his lapel and there it was: the button in the shape of two pink little hands.

"Yes, you are, Sal."

"So, I want to help you, child. I've noticed that you've been drinking, smoking and..."

"And what?"

"You know what?"

"They say it's good for your heart."

We two laughed like two old sisters. Then, looking me in the eye, he said, "What I see is a very lonely *girl* in front of me."

I didn't know what to say and, trying to change the subject, I asked, "Sal, why are you always wearing that button?"

"That's a long story."

"Well, I'd love to hear it."

"Once I had a lover who would tell me I had the coldest little hands he had ever touched. Before he died, he gave it to me. And I saved it."

I immediately started to cry.

"I guess you're right, Sal. I am lonely."

"So it's time you changed, child."

The real estate market in New York was not doing well by the beginning of the eighties. Although I had first thought of the bar being only for fun, it turned out to be my life salvation raft. That was the place I felt most needed, where I went to flirt, cruise and meet new people. Being one of the owners made things easier.

***

"I don't know what to do."

"I don't, either," Diego said as he was pouring me a demitasse of Cuban espresso.

"..."

"But I know who've you been missing," he said, handing me the cup.

"What are you trying to say, Diego?"

"Nelson, I can see why you've been cruising and meeting all those kids at Sal's. It seems to me you're running away from him."

"Who?"

"Have you opened that letter from Brazil?"

"I have."

"So you know that Carlos wrote it."

"Yes. So? How do you know?"

"He wrote me and sent me a carbon copy of that letter also."

"Why?"

"He misses you lots. In that letter, he calls you his only true *Papi*."

"Yes, but Carlos changed so much when he came to this country."

"Did you read the whole letter?"

"Yes."

"What did you feel reading it?"

"I guess I still love that kid. But what should I do?"

"You know what. But, first, I have to tell you something about Carlos."

"Now, *what?*"

"Do you remember the day he ran to my house after you two had that big fight?"

"*Sí.*"

"On the phone, if you remember, you asked

me how his foot was."

"Well, if his foot had stopped bleeding, as I'd told you, why was I going to bring him to the pharmacist?"

"I never thought about that."

"I don't know how you're going to take this. Carlos, at that time, had gotten V.D."

"You see? I was right! He was fooling around..."

"Please. The kid is still hurt and wants to come back. He adores you."

"But why did he do that?"

"Who knows, Nelson. Give'im a second chance, will you?"

"I don't know, Diego."

"Promise me you'll think about it."

"Ok, then."

I did think about it. Five minutes later, I picked up the phone and dialed the Brazilian airline in Manhattan again. Three days later, I was ringing the bell of a huge mansion in Rio.

"Yes?" a voice said firmly and loudly, trying to outdo the barking of two huge German shepherds behind the wooden gate.

"It's me!" I said out loud.

A little window was quickly opened right in the middle of the gate, allowing me to see his beautiful green eyes and the beginning of a big smile. I heard the sound of padlocks being hurriedly unlocked. He finally got it open and throwing himself in my arms, he whispered, "Nelson, my *Papi!*"

I hugged him back and we kissed the longest kiss. I smelled something velvety in the air, the same magical smell that had always followed me. I must say that I was concerned about the neighbors, but the streets were deserted at that time of the day. From the house, I could hear the waves breaking on the shore.

Inviting me to come in, we went straight to his room. It was in the servant's area, in back of the house, where I was almost eaten alive, not by Carlos, but by two shepherd dogs. And, of course, we made love.

"I really want you to hear what I have to propose to you."

"Yes," he said, pouring me a Brazilian coffee espresso.

"I do want you back more than anything. We both should give ourselves a second chance, yes, and see what the future brings."

"Whatever you say, *mi amor.*"

He took a sip of his hot back coffee in the tiniest porcelain demitasse I had ever seen.

"Since we're starting all over. Enough of mutual jealousy and silly suspicions."

Were those lines straight out from a romance novel?

"Yes, Carlos."

"I shall then be yours for the rest of our lives."

He sounded like a sappy, Latin American soap-opera star.

"Let's not exaggerate, *honey.* Let's give it time."

Chapter 15

Year followed year and life with Carlos proved to be wonderful until that scalding August afternoon in 1987. I was rehearsing a new number at the bar with the girls and the piano was being tuned at that same time. Note after note, the sounds of the piano started growing inside my mind by the minute, driving me crazy. Ten minutes of that, the sounds got louder, echoing endlessly inside my head. I also felt an acute pain on my right side, going down my ribs like the claws of a huge crab painfully perforating my body. The tired girls, the out-of-tune piano and the unbearable pain forced me to go home quickly. I took a cab. I just couldn't walk home that day. Carlos was not in and I went straight to our bed. The bright light coming from outside bothered my eyes, but I just had no energy to get up and draw the curtains shut. I got under the covers and fell asleep immediately.

"How are we going to get to Florida?" I asked Mamita, my aunt in Cuba, next to me.

"They say that from the tip of the island, where the Guantánamo Naval Base is we can set sail for Florida easily. The currents are perfect. If we are lucky enough, they will take us to Miami in a matter of two days."

"Mamita, do you think we'll be able to sail on this flimsy homemade raft made out of four tractor inner tubes that we stole from the Cooperative farm in the country?"

"We're just four: Pepe, you father, you and me. It should hold us pretty well, no? It'll carry us to freedom."

"I'm not so sure, Mamita."

"What are you afraid of?"

"Of being eaten alive by those sharks."

"Honey, you're being eaten alive right at this moment, anyway."

"What d'you mean?"

"I don't want to talk about it."

"Please, Mamita, tell me..."

"This pain you've just got..."

"*Sí?*"

"I'm sorry. It's not good news, *hijo*. Do you

want to stay here or try to leave with us?"

"I want to leave, of course, but I don't want this pain, either. Help me, Mamita."

"There's one thing you should do."

"What?"

"You've got to leave with us. No matter what happens. I promise you that you'll find a way out by yourself, Nelson."

Suddenly, I felt the heat from a face next to mine as if the face itself wished to be part of that dream. Then, I heard a voice calling my name from very far away and I just couldn't open my eyes.

"Nelson! Wake up!"

"Huh?"

"I made you chicken soup. What's going on?"

"I'm sick."

"Well, I got that, all right. I've never seen you in bed at this time of day!"

"I am afraid, Carlos."

"Afraid of what?"

"I feel like my body is being eaten alive at this moment."

"Stop talking nonsense. You need to rest."

He left, closing the door behind him. I ate some of the soup and, still smelling it on the nightstand, I closed my eyes and I went back to sleep right away.

"But what if we can't reach the continent?"

"I can assure you that any place is better than this island," Mamita said, looking me in the eye.

"But I don't have to run away, Mamita. My life's going pretty well now. I have a lover who seems to love me dearly, a bar which gives me moments of happiness, and a job that can bring me lots of money depending on the deals I make."

"I know, honey. But deep inside you know that you'll need to break loose from what you've just found out today."

"What is it, Mamita?"

The phone rang three times and I woke up scared. Next, I heard Carlos's steps coming towards the bedroom. Then he knocked on the door and as he opened it, he softly spoke that the girls were on the phone to ask if I was going to the bar that night. I asked Carlos to tell them I wasn't. I needed to rest.

***

I didn't go to work or to the bar for two weeks in a row. I had no energy and the pain seemed to be expanding inside me. Looking myself in the mirror, I panicked, discovering that I had lost a lot of weight. And I had to think of something to tell my friends like, "I'm on a weight-loss program."

Carlos was really concerned with my heath and wouldn't stop bugging me to see a doctor. One night, I promised him I was going to, then tossing in bed, I closed my eyes and was immediately transported to my beloved Cuba once again.

"Nelson, would you like to come to a wedding with me tonight?"

"But, Mamita, aren't we going to the States?"

"We'll go soon. But now, let's have fun."

"I haven't bought anything for the bride or the groom."

"It doesn't matter. The Government has done that for us."

"What did it give the couple as a wedding present?"

"Two crates of beer."

I decided not to go to the wedding and started wandering around my neighborhood. Walking down the street, I found myself on a long, wide avenue leading to the sea. It was very hot and the side streets baked in the sun. Then I saw a red neon sign, which read something that I couldn't make out from the distance, a sentence, a motto. But I was too far away to read it clearly. One thing I knew for sure it consisted of three words: the first started with a big "S," the middle word was extremely short, as if it were connecting the two others, and the third started with a "D."

I was about to read it when I was awakened by the sounds of curtains being drawn open. Carlos, let the sun in and said that I should get up and see a doctor immediately and jokingly he said if I didn't, he was going to divorce me.

***

"How long since you had an X-ray taken, Nelson?"

"A long time ago."

"Do you remember when?"

"Yes, my sister's told me that I was one of the first members of my family to go to the hospital in Cuba, to have his head X-rated."

"What for?"

"I had meningitis when I was two."

"Do you smoke?"

"Yes."

"How many packs a day?"

"Two or three. Depends."

"Drink?"

"Yes."

"A lot?"

"I used to drink a lot more than now," I lied.

"We need to take a picture of your stomach, pancreas and liver. So come back tomorrow and please do not eat anything before that."

"Ok, Doctor."

I returned on the following day and after drinking the most disgusting juice, I was brought to the X-ray room, where I took my shirt off and stood behind the machine. Two minutes later, I was asked to put on my shirt, leave the room and wait for my doctor outside. The results would come out a week later.

***

I was about to sit on a tall stool in my doctor's office, when he came in, producing an X-ray out of a manila envelope and asked me to keep calm. He had bad news: I had cirrhosis of the liver.

Chapter 16

La Habana

7 September 1987

Querido Nelson:

You simply cannot imagine how painful it is to write you this letter. But, as I promised to you over the phone, here it is.

I believe you know about the problem with you father's left arm. With therapy it really got much better, but the poor thing lost his appetite almost completely. Fortunately, feeling so much less pain on his arm made him a little optimistic.

I also have to tell you that it is true that your Mother did not leave him alone one single moment; however, she was constantly bugging him, just like a hammer that doesn't stop banging night and day. Everybody tried to talk some sense into her, but you know your Mother.

After a month in the hospital, he came back home. But at that time, he already knew his fate: the doctors had coldly told him he hadn't much longer to live. When I found out about that, I wanted to send them a bomb as a present. He was really depressed and preferred not to talk. I was lucky when I went to his room (and as you know, he always had a little crush on me which I knew) because on that day he talked to me nonstop. Everyone in the house was hopeful to see him in such good spirits. But, Nelson, that was the last time they saw him giggling and smiling. Two days later, we thought he was going to leave us. He had a thrombosis. He could hardly communicate with us. When he tried talking, his tongue sounded as if it was glued to the roof of his mouth. Bad luck knocked on our family's door. He then became paralyzed.

He was immediately rushed back to the hospital and the disease had spread throughout his brain. Now, writing this letter, I remember him saying many times that his head seemed to be full of water. Heavy. He lived six more days. Before he left us, one day he became conscious. That was the day

I went to visit him. When I entered the room, I found a very cute, young nurse -- extremely platinum blonde -- spoon-feeding him some soup. When I approached -- she was standing by your father and leaning against the bed -- I surreptitiously peeked inside the bowl she held. I don't know what got into me, and started screaming at the little woman to get out of the room at once. She just looked at me as if I had gone mad, in disbelief. When I looked down at the soup, I first thought I'd seen two little frogs freely swimming in the thick liquid. But, dearest Nelson, guess what those "little frogs" really were: nothing but five big, fat snow pea pods floating on the surface.

On that day, he wrote on a piece of paper that he now had to go since he didn't belong to Earth anymore. Tears rolled down his cheeks copiously. Your father was ninety-five years old and that made him a celebrity in itself. His name will be entered on the books of the City Hall not for his more than forty years as a professional journalist, but because he died at that age. He was buried at the Cemetery of Colón on a rainy day.

We ourselves cleaned his body. Enriquito, who is now a father of two robust twin boys, came to the bed and when he ran a comb through your father's hair, there was a shower of thoughts, letters and words. Seeing that on the pillow, one of Enriquito's son, Luisito, who is a very curious little boy, picked up two thoughts and quickly put them in his overall pocket. Nobody could talk him into giving those thoughts back for us to bury them with your father. He saved them as his own treasure.

Mi amor, my regards to everybody over there and receive thousands of kisses from someone who has always loved you very much.

Mamita

Chapter 17

Six months later, I looked like a vampire, afraid of the light of the day. I had lost a lot of weight, and my mustache looked longer because of my bony, wilted face. I looked scary even to myself. Carlos was terrified seeing me like that but, because I decided to try everything he recommended -- natural and macrobiotics food, meditation and even a couple of crystals placed on my forehead -- and he temporarily quit begging me to call either my brother Oswaldo, the little doctor, or my sister Carmela in Florida. I had successfully convinced him that I could get over that without any outside help. His company and love were enough. And although I had fallen very ill, we never stopped making love.

One Saturday afternoon, I invited Diego to come by the house. I was taking a shower when I heard the doorbell. The door was open and from the bathroom, I yelled for him to come in. I heard noises in the living room and then in the kitchen.

"Nelson, I'm making Cuban espresso. Is that alright?

"Sure, honey. Go ahead. I'm dying for a cup."

Wrapping a towel around my head, putting on a robe that matched the towel and lighting a cigarette, I came out of the bathroom, resembling a decrepit Bette Davis.

Diego was browsing through my opera records in the living room when he saw the shower steam slowly oozing out of the bathroom before he saw me. I was already in the room when he finally found me in the middle of so much steam. I noticed he had gotten scared when he saw me ridiculously skinny.

"Sit down, Diego. I've something very serious to tell you."

His face turned pale.

"What is it, Nelson?" he said, handing me a demitasse.

"I went to the doctor six months ago and..."

"Tell me."

"... he said I had cirrhosis."

"Oh, God," he whispered, almost dropping some of the coffee on the couch.

"Don't worry. He also told me that cirrhosis is perfectly curable nowadays."

I knew that Diego would not buy that.

"But how did you get it?"

"I've always enjoyed drinking..."

"Yes, I know, but I've never seen you really drunk."

"To be honest with you, I never drank a lot in front of people, but I guess I secretively became an alcoholic, especially after joining the bar when Carlos left for Brazil. Yes, honey, I drank alone till I used to fall on this very floor."

"What are you going to do?"

"Try to relax as much as I can."

"Work?"

"Fortunately, I have some money saved. Carlos and I will be Ok."

"I'm so sorry, Nelson."

He stood up and came near me for a hug. He put his arms around me and, for a few seconds, I felt totally protected. But then free from his strong, long octopus arms, I felt helpless and small.

"I want you to do me a favor, Diego. Please ask Sal to come here so we can talk about the bar."

"Shall do."

"Thanks."

"Where's Carlos?"

"He went upstate for a show where he and his students are going to demonstrate *Capoeira*. It's a college or something."

"I guess his classes are going well."

"Yes. I'm very happy for him."

"When's he coming back?"

"Tomorrow night."

"You're going to stay here by yourself?"

"Not really. I'll have company. The boys..."

"What boys?"

"Those hunks."

"I don't understand, Nelson."

"My porno videos, silly."

I had a huge collection of porno movies and that's what I was watching almost every night and the B-movies on TV in the wee hours. I had undoubtedly switched day for night.

"I'm staying here tonight."

"Not necessary."

"I insist."

"Ok."

"Dinner?"

"We'll order out."

***

Carlos extended his trip for five more days and I was left alone in the house. I really didn't mind. I didn't feel like going out anyway. The telephone was left untouched, and the answering machine had, at least, thirty messages. I felt sorry for the callers that had forcibly to hear the longest beep they could have possibly ever heard. Food? We had a pantry full of canned food, *chorizos* -- of all kinds and sizes -- bacon, *jamón*, *frijoles*, *papas*, *tortillas*, coffee and endless condiments. The apartment was a complete mess. Clothes, videos and records were scattered all over the place. I didn't even bother to get dressed and had lost total interested in cleaning the apartment. Spoiled food was in the kitchen sink, let alone, in the fridge, which stank like the area reserved for the elephants at a zoo. I just felt like watching TV, and going to my favorite refuge, my bed...

***

"But if we leave from Guantánamo, it's going

to be very easy for the American Coast guards to pluck us from the sea."

"We'll shove off our homemade raft at dusk, so we can both avoid them and the heat of the day."

"Mamita, do you think it's a good idea?"

"Honey, I cannot wait till changes happen on this island anymore. I cannot wait to get a visa to leave Cuba. I'm totally driven to desperation. You were smart enough to leave so long ago. But I can't live like this, Nelson."

"I understand," I said, lowering my head.

"And also, if they catch us, it'll even be better. We won't need to risk our lives in the straits."

"Maybe you're right."

"My only problem now is the language."

"I'll help you with that."

"Really?"

"*Sí.*"

"*Gracias.*"

"Are we ready to go?"

"Almost, Nelson."

***

Bang. Bang. Bang...

I was awakened by the knocks on my bedroom French door that opened onto the patio. At first I could not recognize who was out there. Later I found out that they had jumped the fence that separated the patio from my next-door neighbor's. Slowly, I began making out two silhouettes that kept shouting and waving recklessly to me: Carlos and my brother, the little doctor, who had flown from Maine after Diego telephoned him. That afternoon Diego came by the apartment, he had stolen my address book.

I simply could not get up; I felt as if I had been strapped to the bed. I yelled back that I wanted to be left alone. The knocks on the door were even louder this time. For a while I had the oddest feeling that they were curious looking at me through the glass window of a nursery. They could not understand me and kept pushing the door until it finally opened. The only thing I understood was Carlos's first comment that the whole apartment stank. My brother looked petrified. He came closer to the bed. I then murmured, "Mamita, I have to go back to the house and fetch my things." My brother looked confused. Asking me how I felt, I only turned to the other side and hid my face on the soft pillow. I just didn't feel like talking to anyone, especially my brother whom I hadn't seen for so many years.

I heard Carlos cleaning up in the kitchen.

"Carlos, how long has he been sick?"

"A few months now."

"Why haven't you ever called me?"

"He asked me not to."

"Carlos! Don't you understand? He's ill."

"I know, but I only followed what he wanted me to do."

"You fool."

For the whole afternoon, they kept arguing with each other and trying to get me out of bed. I refused to go to a hospital. They even called a fireman from the firehouse that had no intention of helping them, claiming that it would be against my rights if he carried me out of the bedroom.

"What rights?" Oswaldo screamed. "Can't you see this man is dying?"

Those words hurt me so much. And closing my eyes, in response to my brother, at the top of my lungs, I threw out my chest, "Wait for me, Mamita!"

"He makes no sense. Can't you hear him?"

"If he is not willing to go to a hospital, I can't do anything, sir."

Carlos wouldn't give up trying to persuade me

to go to a hospital. I had no time to waste -- I said to Carlos -- I was crossing the Florida straits very soon.

Carlos was scared. He started to cry and say that I made no sense. He brought his face wet with tears near mine and whispered in my ear, "Where's my lovely *Papi* gone to?"

"I'm not gone yet, Carlos," I said loudly.

"Nelson, please, I beg you. Let us take you to a hospital."

"Only if you wait a few minutes. I have to stop by the house and collect some of my things…"

"Nelson you're in our house. You don't have to go anywhere."

"I certainly do, honey. In the meantime, ring Diego, Dan, Water and Ronald. I want them here to see me leave on the boat. Time is ticking away."

"What are you saying?"

"Please do what I asked you. Then, I will come with you."

A car service was strategically parked outside the apartment. I was so weak that I couldn't even stand. Carlos had to carry me to the car as if I were a baby. I weighed as much as one anyway. My brother followed us closely.

The car ride was making me sick and the radio

was on, bothering me tremendously. I could not help vomiting on the seat, which made me so embarrassed that I started to cry. I could not focus on anything, either. The lights outside passed by us so quickly. Then, full of static, the radio spoke, "If riding a car is making you so sick, d'you really thing you'll be able to sail with us?"

"Mamita! There's only one thing that'd keep me from not going with you: only if you told me that this raft was not seaworthy at all."

"Well, I believe it is, see? Two inner tubes piled on two others with wooden planks separating them. The contraptions have been firmly wrapped with strong, thick sisal."

"So, Mamita, I'm sure I won't get much sicker than riding this car."

"We're almost ready to set out."

"Wonderful."

I only remember the car's wheels screeching away after depositing us right on the sidewalk before the hospital. Oswaldo rushed in front of us to ask for a wheel chair. And that was the most humiliating thing for me: have to ride in one of those. But I simply could not walk and Carlos was not allowed to carry me into the building. That was the law.

We went straight to the ER which was crowded like the beach near Havana with its thousands of would-be rafters. I thought that here was the place where we were all supposed to sail from. I then came to the conclusion that Mamita was delaying our departure exactly because she wanted me to come here. That was part of the plan. But I wondered why she hadn't told me before.

Oswaldo and Carlos went to talk to a very cute young nurse, extremely platinum blonde, at the window, who apparently was concerned only if I had health insurance or not. I did. However, mine did not cover all expenses. Oswaldo told her that he himself was a doctor and he would fix those things later. Carlos looked desolate. With my head down, my chin touching my collar bone, I kept my eyes closed. I was exhausted and had to rest for the coming departure.

***

Two hours later, I was wheeled into another room, leaving Carlos and Oswaldo back in the ER. They waved goodbye. I then saw Carlos hugging Oswaldo, leaning his forehead against Oswaldo's shoulder, sobbing.

A very bright, naked fluorescent lamp hanging from the ceiling right on top of me illuminated the spacious, blue-tiled room. I could hear bits of conversation here and there. Four doctors examined me at once.

"What do you think?"

"We'll definitely need a CAT-SCAN."

"Right now?"

"If not now, in a couple of hours."

"What next?"

They touched my body as if they were looking for something they four had lost inside me. I screamed in pain. When they started pushing their hands against the area of my liver, I called desperately for *Papi*. I opened my eyes and noticed that the team of doctors didn't even bother, mechanically continuing their check up.

"Mr. Nelson, what are you feeling right now?"

"Desperation."

The looked puzzled.

"I want to get out of this island. I can't stand it anymore."

They looked even more perplexed this time.

"We need to know what's hurting you."

"*Ouch.* That really hurt."

By now they were convinced that I was conscious; though, perhaps slightly incoherent.

"Mr. Nelson, we'll unfortunately have to insert a needle in your spine. Are you allergic to anything?"

"No! let me go!"

The words were hardly out of my mouth when I felt a cold needle easily piercing my skin. My flesh felt just like an old thin, wrinkled piece of paper. I had never felt so much pain in my life.

"Nelson?"

"*Sí?*"

"Be brave, honey. We'll be out of this shortly. I promise."

"Mamita! Why is it taking us so long to leave?"

"Soon, honey. Very soon. Once again, be brave. *Te adoro.*"

"I love you, too."

A woman doctor smiled at me. I guess she thought I had said that to her. In fact, I hated that woman doctor. I hated the whole team of doctors who were only interested in trespassing my own body, so to speak. I hated them all.

***

All of a sudden, I was alone in the room. I believe two hours had passed when they came back, bringing, according to them, good news.

I was totally scared of them. They looked like a flock of hungry, crazy seagulls with their overalls flapping like gigantic wings.

"Mr. Nelson, your marrow liquid looks OK."

"Good."

"But we'll have to keep you here until you feel better."

"Please tell those guys outside to go home."

"Who are they, Mr. Nelson?"

"The older man is my brother. And the kid is my lover."

***

The next morning, Carlos and Oswaldo came to visit. I had already been hooked up to two intravenous tubes, and felt numbed by the pain killers they had given me the night before. They looked scared when they saw my butter-colored face and my sunken eyes. Pretending that everything was fine, Carlos started smoothing the blanket at the foot of the bed. He looked so sad. My brother said a weak hello and went straight to the window, brushing his cheeks with the back of his hand.

"Carlos, I want you to try to find my will."

"Hush-hush," he said.

"It's necessary, Carlos."

"I don't want you to think about those things now. You should think about getting better."

"It's damn important."

"OK, Nelson. Don't speak. Try to sleep."

"I think it's under the bathroom sink."

"All right, honey."

"Oswaldo?"

"Yes, Nelson. I'm here."

"I want you to call Carmela and tell her to come. I'm leaving soon."

"Good. Carlos and I cleaned the whole apartment. You'll love it."

"I'm serious. I am leaving."

"Hush," Carlos sounded as if had something glued to the inside of his throat.

"Oswaldo, d'you remember Mamita?"

"Of course, I do."

"She's told me we're leaving the island pretty soon."

"Nelson, Mamita is in Cuba!"

"But aren't we all?"

He broke into tears and left the room. Carlos kept running a comb through my hair asking me to go to sleep.

"I can't, Carlos. I'm wasting time. I need to get ready."

"OK, *Papi.*"

"I'm not scared, dear."

"You shouldn't, anyway. You're getting outta here shortly."

"I know."

Chapter 18

The doctors kept doing exams on my head on the following weeks. It felt as if they were rummaging inside my head: three CAT-SCANS in only twelve days. By then, I was hooked to three intravenous tubes and taking a mound of oral medications daily. I kept losing weight by the hour, throwing up everything. I tried eating and the annoying, constant diarrhea wouldn't leave me alone. But the worst of it was the fatigue. I was exhausted from the minute I woke in the morning until I closed my eyes to sleep.

One evening, when the visiting hours were over and Carlos, Oswaldo, Diego, Dan had left, I stayed up, looking at the door to pass the time and see what was going on in the corridor. Suddenly, Mamita showed up, bringing me a red felt cap. She asked me to put it on and follow her: we were going out for a walk. I was still very weak and needed to sit down a little bit. I felt dizzy when I tried to get up. We stayed in the waiting room where a group of patients was talking, playing dominoes, eating cake and watching TV. The picture on the screen rolled up and down endlessly.

Mamita and I were getting close to the hospital entrance now, and I thought that if we walked past the guards, nobody would catch us. That's what fortunately happened. Nobody prevented me from getting out. On the corner of the long and wide avenue where the majestic hospital stood, we made a left and there we were: right on Prado Promenade! *Mi querida Havana!* I was floating on a cloud of happiness. Mamita grabbed my hand and we ran to a nice little restaurant at Fraternidad Park. We sat at a sidewalk table, drinking beer and nibbling on cheese cut in cubes.

"Mamita, I can't eat the hospital food."

"Too bland, huh?"

"Yes. Carlos's been bringing me lunch. Mamita, should we bring some for our trip?"

"Of course not, silly. We can't bring anything but us. We can't overload the raft."

"Carlos could make us some food."

"No, honey."

"Should we order now?"

"Let's."

'I'd love to have apricot with apple."

"Baby food? I'll have that too."

The waiter then brought us the mushy food on two nice china plates.

"Where's *Papi*?" I asked, taking a bite of the food.

"You'll see him when the time comes."

"What about Pepe?"

"He'll be there, too."

Next, we walked towards the sea. I smelled hints of salt in the air. We took la Rampa, La Copellia and El Malecon. As we kept chatting, we were approaching this rundown hotel. I knew I had been there before. I recognized the area. Mamita wouldn't stop talking. I was getting nervous with every step we took towards the building. We were getting nearer and nearer...

There was the neon sign! I had finally come to it and I could easily read it now: the first word starting with an "S" was totally burned out and it read "SOCIALISM." Socialism was burned out, all right. The connecting word was also unlit and it was "OR." I had more chills running up and down my back. Seeing me so pale, Mamita asked if I wanted to sit down on the curb for a while. I said no, but it was obvious that I was about to pass out. I knew that it was not a sentence; it was, without a doubt, Fidel's motto. The third one was the only word fully brightly lit. And in enormous red script, it read: "DEATH!"

***

"Mr. Nelson, wake up," said the nurse on the night shift, shaking my arm.

"Huh?"

"It's time for your medication."

I half-opened my left eyelid and her platinum blonde hair shone like a car's bumper, hurting my eye.

"Let me sleep. I don't want it."

"I'll leave the tablets here on the nightstand, then."

"Fine. G'night."

"Nightie-night."

***

"Nelson, wake up."

"Huh?"

"It's time for your medication."

I opened my eyes and missing my cheek, Carlos kissed me right on my left eye.

"*Ouch.* Let me sleep."

"Nelson, you didn't take your medicine last night."

"Nah."

"Brat! Did you buzz the nurse? Where was she?"

"Dunno. Maybe dying her hair... *Coño*, lemme sleep."

"Dr. Millman is here," Carlos announced.

"G'morning, Mr. Nelson."

I totally ignored her. I hated her guts.

"Do you know what day's today?"

When we went through her routine, and I first kept quiet. For three weeks in a row now, she would ask me the same questions whenever she stopped in my room. Day or night.

"Do you know who's the current president of the United States?"

"Fidel."

"Beg your pardon?"

"George."

"Bush?"

"No. Washington."

"George's the vice, Mr. Nelson. Maybe if you made an effort... I'll give you a clue. He was an actor."

"Oh, yes, the clown president."

She blushed a little bit. Maybe she had voted for him, huh?

"Ronald McDonald."

"No," she hissed out in a very disappointing way.

"Got it. Reagan."

"Correct."

What was she doing? Was this a hospital or a popular TV quiz show?

"Mr. Nelson, could you spell world backwards to me?"

"*O-d-n-u-m.*"

For three weeks, every time she asked me to spell that word, she would not get my answer. If Carlos luckily happened to be in the room, she would ask him what I meant. And poor Carlos, rolling his eyes, would tell her that I had just correctly spelled world backwards, but in *Spanish!*

"We'll be starting a battery of tests tomorrow morning, Mr. Nelson. *Please be ready.*"

I took her last sentence as a code, since she somehow and eerily sounded just like Mamita.

***

More CAT-SCANS. More blood transfusions. More marrow liquid taken. More pain. And the number of medicine bottles increased day after day, taking the whole space on my nightstand. I honestly could not keep track of all those pills whose brands consisted of only a few acronyms.

A week after Dr. Millman had told me about those exams, she came into the room and we went through the same questions. This time, a thick stack of paper of notes and graphs was clamped to the clipboard she carried.

"Mr. Nelson. We've been doing a lot of tests and we've also done an experiment with your blood and marrow liquid."

I started to shake. My feet and hands were quickly frozen.

"It seems to us that the meningitis you had when you were two years old, as you've told us, has played an important and, unfortunately, bad role on your present physical condition."

Carlos sank into a chair near the bed. Reaching for my bony hand, his big green eyes were teary.

"Do I have meningitis?"

"We don't think so. I just want to let you know that what we've found in your blood is a total new universe for us, doctors. For the field of Medicine as well. This disease is very new and we do not know much about it. We've been doing something considered very advanced, though. We've been counting your T-cells every single day."

And after explaining to me what the purpose of those cells in the blood was, I was totally confused: were those disguised instructions for my trip with Mamita, Pepe and *Papi*? They were too complicated for my burned-out mind. I wished Mamita had been there so that she could easily explain it to me better.

"So, all the doctors, who've come to visit you these past three months, came to the conclusion that..."

***

Mamita, where are you? *Papi*, help me! Pepe, get me outta here!

***

I only saw Dr. Millman's lips moving soundless as if she were in a silent movie. Carlos quickly stood up and came to hug me. When she had left the room, closing the door behind her, Carlos started to sob uninterruptedly.

Dr. Millman had no sooner finished telling me that I had been infected with the most-talked-about four-letter word plague in this century, than, tear-eyed myself, at the top my lungs and in response to my fate, I screamed out the most-spoken four-letter curse word in the entire English language.

Chapter 19

I now spent long hours listening to La Bohème over and over again on the Walkman I had asked Carlos to bring me in the hospital. That was my only pastime; I had once and for all quit reading. When my friends came to visit, they all looked at my scary face, soundlessly mimicking Mimi in the opera. I never told any of them that I had always, all my life, deep inside, felt that *I* was Mimi. And being trapped in that bed for so long proved to be that I was damn right: I was Mimi.

I had no energy left, making use of a mask hooked to an oxygen tank beside my bed. My liver was hugely swollen, and the disease had clearly taken hold of my body, which was shrinking by the minute. I had the impression that the disease had taken over me just like Fidel had taken over Cuba. It had spread throughout my body in less than six months.

My sister came from Florida as well as *el americanito*. My brother Oswaldo's children and wife also came to the hospital. Sal visited me almost every day. And to my surprise, Ronald and Walter wouldn't skip a week without stopping by.

Feeling much better, one day, more precisely July 10, 1988, I tiptoed out of the room. It was easy.

Taking the mask off my face, I laid it on the nightstand, which had Carlos's countless crystals plus New Age tapes that were supposed to give me strength and courage. I tenderly touched a couple of stones for luck and walked out...

Mamita was anxiously waiting for me at the end of the corridor. She had her pants rolled up to her knees and walked barefoot, appropriately dressed for sailing. I took a deep breath and ran to her. When my lungs were filled up with air, I heard the high beep from the machine next to the headboard of the bed. Mamita and I hugged and kissed on the cheeks. Dr. Millman began to ask me her boring questions.

***

"Time to go?" I asked.

"Yes", Mamita answered with a winning smile on her face.

***

I took another breath while Dr. Millman kept asking me how many fingers I saw in her hand. I no longer felt like answering her. Carlos's face was near mine and I breathed in his own breath.

I was not scared at all. I didn't even care if the raft was going to be sturdy enough, or if the sharks were salivating underwater, ready to eat us alive. I only wanted to leave that hospital so badly. Carlos kept calling me *Papi*. And I, at the end of the corridor, saw my father appear, as if my magic.

***

"*Papi!*"

"*Hijo!*"

"I'm so glad you're here."

We hugged and kissed.

"So am I, *hijo mio*. So am I..." he said in a very clear voice, lowering his head.

"I missed you so much."

"I'm sorry, *hijo*. *Perdóname*. Forgive me for being such a pigheaded old man. I missed our letters... I also missed you so..."

"Hush-hush. It's OK, father. Hush... We're here together now."

***

I felt the cold sensation of a cotton ball, wet with alcohol, being rubbed against my left, blue arm's vein. Two seconds later, I felt the burning sting of the needle, entering my arm.

***

"Mamita, where's Pepe?"

"See that young man squatting behind the raft?"

"That's *him*?"

I ran the palm-shaded and whipped-cream beach towards the raft. I couldn't believe how energetic I was. The machines in the room beeped continuously; their tiny bulbs, blinking.

"Pepe!" I screamed.

***

Carlos heard that and instinctively whispered in my ear that he was Carlos, not Pepe, who, at that moment, before me, was wearing heavy theatrical makeup.

***

And noticing that I was looking at his face so inquisitively, Pepe proudly said that from now on he would do whatever he pleased. He didn't mind what people thought about him anymore. He was leaving at last in search of freedom.

***

"Nelson!"

By now Carlos was shaking me, almost on top of the bed. Diego had to pull him down by the arm. The kid wouldn't stop crying and calling my name.

***

"Father, aren't you scared?"

"Not at all, *hijo*. This is exactly what I've been wishing for the longest time: to be with you, no matter where we're heading for."

"Nelson!"

"Yes, Mamita."

"D'you think you've got enough strength to help us push the raft into the water?"

"Of course."

"So, honey. This is it!"

***

Carlos screamed my name in pain when he saw the hospital machine producing a continuous line on the monitor. At that very moment, while the machine kept drawing its cold, green, straight line, Mamita, Pepe, *Papi* and I had just finally climbed on top of the raft, trying to balance ourselves. The waves were smooth, and the frothy water felt good on my legs. For the first time in six months, this was the first time they were being bathed by water. The enchanting sapphire waves carried us easily to the open sea.

"Nelson!" Carlos screamed from the shore.

"Farewell, my love," I screamed back.

He didn't hear me.

Chapter 20

Addio senza rancor, as Mimi would say. Farewell without bitterness. Yes, without any grudges! You can be sure, my love, I certainly did not regret a thing I did; on the contrary, I've always had the fullest and happiest life one can have. Why should I now feel hatred towards life? So, please don't be sad...

And before I go back to my never-ending trip over the waters of Florida straits, I want to say one last thing: a year and ten days from that day, Carlos and I were reunited. Yes, we had never stopped making love which eventually resulted in our meeting but, at this time, in a small and very heavy metal box, packed inside an indigo-blue canvas bag. And following my will to the letter, our friends Diego and Dan, sitting side by side on an airplane, flew to Rio, carrying us. Our ashes were inside that box.

From the rocks of Leme, near Copacabana

beach where we had first met, our dear friends released us into the air...

I finally came to find out what that smell, which had followed me all my life was... The moment our mixed ashes hit the seawater, they gave off a strange perfume, the very strange perfume of that little and so complicated thing we simply call... *love*.

Made in the USA
Columbia, SC
20 September 2018